JENNY'S
BACKDOOR
LUST

BETTY BOWMAN

Jenny's Backdoor Lust

Past Venus Press
London 2009

Past Venus Press
is an imprint of
Erotic Review Books

ERB, 31 Sinclair Road,
LONDON W14 0NS
Tel: +44 (0) 207 371 1532
Email: enquiries@eroticprints.org
Web: www.eroticprints.org
© 2009 MacHo Ltd, London UK

Illustrations by Michael Faraday

ISBN : 9781904989639

Printed and bound in the UK by Cox & Wyman Ltd

Jenny's
Backdoor Lust

Betty Bowman

PROLOGUE

By day, Castle Strathblane stood proud in all its splendour, an ancient Scottish Highland legend preserved in stone and mortar. Nestling by the shores of a perfect little freshwater loch, its stark shape loomed dramatically against the wild beauty of purple, heather-clad hills. And now, by night, its crenelated battlements were silhouetted against a dark blue starry sky, and its towers, turrets and roofs glinted in a full, silvery moon. Down the centuries, generations of the same proud, aristocratic family had lived within its thick, fortified walls but now the last of its line had been reduced to the status of a lowly innkeeper, taking in rich foreigners as 'paying guests'. However, George, 15th Earl of Drymuir, was a shrewd businessman and knew just how to market his asset, which often featured in both American and European travel magazines as a superb honeymoon destination, a haven famous for its natural beauty and tranquillity.

Somewhere inside the castle, an old grandfather clock struck twice and from the other side of the loch, an owl hooted as if in reply.

A flashlight flickered briefly at a window on the third floor. It moved on to the next window and then, at the corner of the castle, the lights came on in a large room.

"I say, Johnny-boy, isn't it a bit risky? I mean, lights and all that?" The question came from the older of two men as he gazed somewhat apprehensively down at the girl who seemed, despite his concerns, to be in a deep slumber.

John McAlister sighed. Did he always have to reassure his older cousin?

"You should know me better than that, George. She won't wake up until I tell her to. Watch." He laid down the camera case he was carrying and lifted the covers from the reclining girl's body.

Lord Drymuir's breath whistled out of him in one lewd groan when he saw the full ripe contours of the girl's lush young body. The dark blue silken nightdress had crept up to mid thigh, and the left shoulder strap had slipped down revealing a luscious mound of flesh the size and shape of a ripe melon. John McAlister simply reached forward and pulled the bodice down until it revealed the pale brown areola and nipple. "Watch," he ordered again. Taking the nipple between his thumb and forefinger, he cruelly tweaked it. The girl did not stir, but the nipple — coming alive at his touch — became erect.

"Watch," McAlister repeated, and lifted the hem of the girl's nightie to uncover the gentle curving mound of Venus between her legs and its luxuriant growth of silky black pubic hair. He parted the young bride's legs and, using his right arm under her knees, raised them until the soft pink lips of her vagina could be seen. McAlister glanced over at Lord Drymuir and laughed, not unkindly, at the rapidly breathing older man. Slowly, he placed the tip of his middle finger against his thumb and then flicked at the small bud of her clitoris. The girl remained motionless, but a low moan of lust was wrenched from Lord Drymuir's throat.

McAlister dropped the girl's legs; they remained spread lewdly out with the pink, slightly wrinkled inner lips just open... the entrance to her vagina was completely exposed, defenceless.

"Satisfied?" he asked with a knowing look.

Lord Drymuir trembled in eagerness. "Oh my, yes!" he said hurriedly. "Such a beautiful young creature. Such a fine, tight little cunt! I can hardly wait to pay a visit there." He placed his camera on the chair.

John McAlister glanced at the older man and smiled as he thought to himself, "The old goat's really got the horn tonight."

And why not? McAlister knew his older cousin's proclivities — as well he should, having bought a half-share in the family pile over seven years ago. And since then the two cousins had schemed and plotted to enjoy an almost unlimited supply of innocent female flesh. George Drymuir, at sixty-two years of age, liked his women young, helpless, and tearfully innocent. Most important, however, the scheme the two cousins operated was practically foolproof. There had been no repercussions during the seven years; there was no reason why there should ever be any in the future. John shared his cousin's depraved tastes; he, too, liked young brides — newly married, with the odour of the wedding ceremony's sanctity still clinging to them like the scent of fresh orange blossom. And what better place to get them than at a honeymoon hotel, a romantic old castle, where eager young brides came to be deflowered by their adoring husbands.

"These women," Lord Drymuir had earlier explained unnecessarily, "present a great challenge to men like us. Young, arrogant, proud, and sure of their undying love for their new husbands, they have to be humbled — almost broken in spirit — before they can be taught to crawl to a real master's feet."

Now as George Drymuir watched the sleeping girl, he began to feel a familiar awesome power growing in his loins. The sheer silk gown, above the girl's waist, showed the curved white plain of her belly and the mysterious declivity of her navel. Her pubic hair was like soft black down, and the swollen, fleece-lined vaginal slit was an open invitation to a warm and heavenly tunnel. His eyes alighted on the contours of her buttocks and then moved up over the rising and falling of her breasts. He could see the small nipple still standing proudly erect. Although his throat was dry, his mouth watered. He was impatient to get his teeth and hands on those magnificent mounds of young, almost virginal flesh and to twist, tease, massage, and bite them until they became unbearably trembling volcanoes of passion struggling to erupt.

"Hurry, John," he snapped, not taking his eyes from the girl. "Let's start with the pictures!"

"In a moment. Wait until I get the camera on the tripod." A few moments later, McAlister grunted his satisfaction with the setup and said, "OK."

The thought of those young, almost untouched lips mewling and begging in passion brought a rock-like hardness to the earl's penis. The blood pounded painfully throughout its throbbing length, and he could sense droplets of thick, clear pre-orgasmic fluid already beginning to ooze from its urethral opening.

"All right," McAlister directed, "stand close to her and start unbuttoning your trousers."

The Earl of Drymuir opened the fly of his trousers. His large prick, almost eight inches long and of broad diameter, leapt out like a hungry predator suddenly released from its cage. There was a bright flash of light as McAlister snapped his first picture. Hastily, Drymuir dropped his trousers and underpants. Another flash, together with the sound of film being wound on the next exposure.

"Keep going," McAlister commanded. "I'll shoot as you go along."

Lord Drymuir hesitated now for the first time; he glanced apprehensively toward McAlister. "Are you positive she's completely out of it, old boy?"

McAlister sighed in exasperation and walked over to the bed. He stared intently down at the girl.

"Amanda... Amanda, can you hear?" he asked in a flat tone of voice.

"Yes." The monosyllable was quite flat, without any inflection.

"Amanda... you are with your husband. Open your eyes, Amanda." He pulled Lord Drymuir over alongside her. "See, Amanda. This is your husband, Derek. Say 'hello' to Derek."

The girl blinked, then smiled and said in a loving voice, "Hello, Derek."

"Amanda, you will do anything your husband asks. You'll do it because you love him, and you know it will give him great pleasure. And you, too, will feel much pleasure from him when he makes love to you... so very much pleasure."

She was silent only a second, then she nodded her head woodenly and said, without blinking, "I will do anything my husband asks... it will be a pure pleasure."

"Satisfied?" McAlister asked the older man.

Lord Drymuir eagerly nodded his head. McAlister went back to his camera.

The randy aristocrat squeezed the thick foreskin back from his painfully throbbing penis and bared his teeth as he advanced toward the girl again. The proud young bitch was totally at his mercy. He had heard her giggling as she talked to her husband about him earlier that evening. She had said, "That Lord Drymuir's a dirty old man. A nice, rich, dirty old man, but a dirty old man nonetheless. Did you see the way he looked at me during dinner?" Well, the huge cudgel he held in his hand was a great equalizer between the generations. He'd teach her. He'd see if she still called him a dirty old man when his prick was rammed deep between those creamy white thighs of hers and its head buried far up inside her tight, quivering little cunt.

He was only dimly aware of McAlister taking another photo. The lust was upon him and it was all he could do to keep from leaping on her like some starving wild animal leaps upon its prey. But his common sense prevailed. The pictures, the ones that would bring her crawling to him in abject, hopeless, desperation and insure his and McAlister's future safety, still had to be taken.

"Amanda, dear," he intoned. "Turn your head toward me."

"Yes, Derek," she answered, and her head turned on the pillow.

"Amanda, it would give your husband great pleasure if you kissed and sucked on his penis... as much pleasure as it gives you when he nibbles at your breast."

A troubled expression crossed the girl's face. She hesitated.

Alarmed and wide-eyed, Lord Drymuir turned silently towards the photographer. McAlister merely shook his head and put his finger to his mouth, signalling that he should say nothing.

On the bed, the girl trembled and then, almost as if she were frightened of being bitten by it, reached out her hand toward Lord Drymuir's cock. The old man grinned in triumph and moved forward until the straining organ was almost touching her lips. "Open your mouth, Amanda."

She did as she was instructed, and the smooth, throbbing tip slipped partially through her stretched lips and came to rest against her bared teeth. The soft flesh of her ripe, full lips closed down about the head. There was a flash of light as McAlister took the picture.

Against his cock, Lord Drymuir could feel the hot air exhaling from her nostrils, and could feel her innocent young tongue quivering in ignorance against the instrument in her mouth.

"Delicious," he muttered, "simply delicious. Suck a little and nibble a little, dear." He began moving his hips back and forth as McAlister came in with another camera for a closeup. Several small droplets of pre-come had seeped from Lord Drymuir's cock and had lubricated her mouth that was surrounding its head. Looking down directly at her face, he could see a small stream of glistening saliva and the man's thick, clear fluid running out of the corner of her mouth. Again, for just a moment, the animal heat came upon him. He wanted to shoot his full load down her sweet young gullet... wanted to see her larynx jiggling up and down as she attempted to gulp it down; he could picture it — his cum would spurt out of her mouth, into her hair, and run like a white hot flow of lava across her breasts and down her belly. The mental image goaded him into a sudden frantic motion and he was uncontrollably battering his cock down her choking throat, the girl was gasping for air and clawing at his buttocks when McAlister grinned nastily and said, "Easy, Your Lordship. We still have a few pictures to take, remember?"

Lord Drymuir reluctantly removed his cock from her mouth. He had come so close... so very close. He stood there breathing deeply as he sought to regain his composure. Finally he sighed and said, "That was beautiful, Amanda. Now your husband will repay pleasure for pleasure."

He reached down and removed the remaining strap of her gown, and stared hungrily at the breast. With a low moan of lust, his hot eager lips fastened like a leech to it. There was another flash of light as he used his fingertips to tease the other nipple.

Beneath his lips, he heard a low groan of pleasure from the girl. She placed both hands gently and possessively behind his head. Lord Drymuir glanced over and grinned in victory at McAlister. His lips went back to work, and his other hand dropped until it found the moist hot cavern at the junction of her thighs. He used his finger — as though it were a violin bow — to slide across the length of her vaginal lips. "Oh... oh," she purred.

Amanda began to breath more rapidly as the sensations mounted in her body. Lord Drymuir used his thumb and forefinger to tease her gently pulsating clitoris; this resulted in a low, almost animalistic moaning, "Ohhhh... Derek... that feels wonderful. Bite me — rub me harder!"

George Drymuir suddenly crawled onto

the bed and crouched on all fours over the helpless young body. "Amanda, raise your legs and put them up over my shoulders," he commanded. The girl paused, as if not understanding the instructions, but a moment later subserviently bent her legs at the knees and spreading her legs wide raised and placed her calves up over his shoulders. Lord Drymuir pushed her knees back against her chest; her glorious, upturned sex, already secreting a shiny, clear lubricant, was on generous display — unprotected and vulnerable to any attack. His mouth watered in anticipation as he gazed rapturously down at the palpitating little pussy. A thin line of spittle drooled from the corner his slack, open mouth as he lecherously ogled the open slit of her cunt: it ran down from middle of the dark fur at the base of her smooth white belly to the tight, pale brown anal pucker between the full rounded spheres of her buttocks. He could wait no longer to feast down between her thighs. His head lowered, his mouth opened, and his tongue — wet and healthily pink — came into action.

The girl gasped. "Oh... oh... Derek! You mustn't, please, don't do that! Oh..." She jerked as his lips encompassed and began sucking at the soft hair-lined opening. His skilful, experienced tongue flickered gently, like maddening butterfly's wings, against the bud-like clitoris, which was visibly throbbing.

"Ohhh... Derek..." Her hands came down and pressed against both sides of his head; it was as though she didn't know whether to push him away or force his tongue and face even deeper into the moist pit of her throbbing cunt. Now his tongue had begun seeking entry into the vaginal passage itself. It flicked in and out rapidly, little licks and little strokes of passion that penetrated almost two inches. The girl's hands fell loosely from his head as she groaned and began to rotate her hips in an effort to get his tongue in deeper.

Lord Drymuir was an expert at this sort of thing. He had been ever since a lesson in its finer arts by his father's fiery French mistress: her present to him on his sixteenth birthday. The pupil had proved more than proficient and his teacher had been happy to extend her tutelage by many more mutually enjoyable lessons.

Suddenly, Drymuir withdrew the tongue and his mouth from her now responsive pudenda. Amanda groaned again, this time in disappointment, but only for a second, for his tongue had begun working again; its soft flicking tip made circles around the quivering, erect clitoris, and his lips sucked, drawing the organ deeper into the hot saliva-filled cavern of his mouth. Then he abruptly changed techniques again. Like a thirsty dog lapping water, he now flattened his tongue and used its width to lick the entire length of her wet, rotating cuntal slit. Amanda's loud moans of pleasure turned almost into a scream of delight when his tongue, changing shape again, traced a pattern of fire past the swollen flaps of her inner cuntlips and kept going down, down, to make a lewd, flicking entry into the tight, puckered little ring of her anus.

Now flashes from the camera — like a summer electrical storm — continued to brighten the room.

Lord Drymuir was oblivious to them now. He had the snooty little bitch going; she squirmed and panted like a helpless puppet under his tongue. Soon he would stop again and she'd be so hot that she would beg him to continue. She was completely at his mercy. Her mewls drove his tongue faster and faster as it licked its way up and down the now clasping lips of her cunt. She was almost there; he could tell by the wild contractions of her vaginal muscles. His muffled laughter came as her hands desperately clawed at his head — seeking to drive his tongue further and further into her. The hot, happy bitch, he thought; she doesn't realize that what she really wants right now is some hard cock. She'll be begging for it within seconds.

He pulled his face away, tormenting her. Amanda's face was wildly contorted in what appeared to be pain. She cried, and it was a moaning plea, "No... Derek. Please, Derek... keep going."

Lord Drymuir let her force him this time, and she did so, frantically, pressing his mouth against her hungrily quivering vagina. His lips rounded and covered the clasping viscous opening, and he thrust his tongue deep into it. Her thighs closed convulsively around either side of his moving head. On his inward strokes, he could feel her deeper vaginal muscles sucking and milking at his tongue as if they sought to rip it out by the roots and devour it. Amanda's legs had found leverage against his back and she pushed down until he could barely breathe. With tongue deep in her vagina, he used the tip of his nose to titillate the tiny throbbing clitoris. Every muscle in the girl's body seemed to be as taut as a steel cable. The tendons of her neck stood out as she tried to raise her head to look down her naked body and see what he was doing.

"Oh! Ahhh? Unnnh?," she began, as if questioning exactly what was happening to her. Then she screamed, "Ohhhh... Ah... mmmmm... I'm coming, darling! Ohhh, I'm c-c-co...ming!" Her body thrashed from side to side, her legs splayed open releasing his head, and her feet beat a tattoo of wild abandoned lust against the crumpled sheets.

Lord Drymuir didn't even glance over

toward McAlister. He could stand it no longer. Even as the girl was thrashing and twitching involuntarily in the throes of her orgasm, he grabbed her flailing legs behind the knees again and shoved them roughly back against her shoulders. His long rigid prick was placed against the visibly throbbing lips of her cunt.

"Now I'm going to fuck you until you can't walk, you little strumpet!" he said through gritted teeth, and suddenly began pushing forward. The elastic rimmed tightness resisted his huge circumference for only a moment, then rapidly gave way to his unrelenting pressure. Down, down, down, the pulsating white rod drove.

Amanda tried to pull back from his attack. "No, Derek," she whimpered, "darling, you're hurting me."

Lord Drymuir paused. The contractions of her cunt continued to squeeze at the head of his cock; he hadn't realized the girl's pussy was so tight. It fit his prick like a very tight leather glove, and he thought with considerable glee that the girl undoubtedly had been a virgin on her wedding night, just two days before.

She obviously had never had a prick this deep into her before, he gloated to himself, as he watched her from above with a libidinous smirk on his face. Her lips had curled back from her teeth in a pretty snarl of lust-pain.

Pleading, incoherent whimpers of pain came from deep within her throat and a frown of anguish distorted her pretty face.

Abruptly, he could stand it no more. He rammed forward giving her all he had in one great implacable thrust; his huge expanded cock sunk in all the way to his pubic hair, and his balls — the size of large plums — slapped hard against her uplifted buttocks. Her eyes flew wide open, staring into space, her legs jerked out wide on either side of his body as she kicked futilely into the air and screamed, "Oh, God! You're killing me, Derek. Please!" It was a scream wrenched from the depths of her tortured womb.

As though demented, Lord Drymuir screwed her brutally down into the soft mattress — pounding into her with the uncontrollable fury of a winter's storm.

McAlister watched with some amusement as the old goat went about his business of ravishing the helpless girl. He had already shot two rolls of film on his tripod camera and had expended another two rolls on closeups. The girl's face was too distorted by pain to take any photos at the moment, but McAlister knew that her expression would change once her tight young pussy got used to the old man's cock. You had to hand it to him, he thought in admiration as he watched the white pistoning rod being driven relentlessly into the girl's tightly clenched vagina. My cousin Drymuir's hung like a small stallion.

Even as McAlister was musing upon Drymuir's sexual prowess, the girl's body seemed to be reacting differently. Her groans of pain came less often now; they sounded altered — questioning, perhaps. Once, when Lord Drymuir had pulled his prick out about six inches and then driven it inward with one masterful stab, the girl had moaned and an unmistakable flash of pleasure crossed her contorted face.

And moments later, there was an almost imperceptible change in activity on the bed. McAlister saw it first, simply a small motion on the part of the girl as she pushed up to meet a downward thrust. The rest came rapidly; the young bride's eyes were beginning to glaze in pleasure, and a pink tongue had crept out of her mouth to rest quivering on her lower lip. It presented a lustful picture; McAlister lost no time in capturing her lewd changing expression on film.

Now the girl was moving, experimentally rotating her hips and putting her arms around Lord Drymuir's midriff. Not satisfied with this, she reached down and cupped his buttocks in the palms of her hands and began of her own volition forcing him deeper into her.

Lord Drymuir could hardly contain himself

as he felt her abdomen begin moving up and down in time to the thrusts of his hardened cock. The contracting muscles inside her pussy were hungrily at work massaging and sucking at the inflated head. With each withdrawal of his long white cock, the pink lips of the vagina pulled and milked at the instrument. The girl was evidently one of Nature's trollops, he thought in glee, as her quivering body pumped up and down on the rigid penis fusing the two bodies together.

McAlister had begun to feel some excitement growing within himself as he watched the girl strain against his older cousin. When she raised her ass from the mattress, he could see the little brown puckered anal entrance already covered with trickling exudate. And he thought happily, eagerly: You're next, little asshole, you're next! I've got just the thing for you. McAlister took photographs of it all, capturing on film the utter abandon of her labours and the half-crazed smile of lust playing across her taut lips. She was moving even faster than the old man now, and thrusts had become more violent as she desperately sought her second orgasm. Above the tortured creaking of the bed and the almost obscene slap of flesh against flesh, McAlister could actually hear the wet sluicing sounds of her juicy, voracious pussy as it reluctantly relinquished its hold on the lustfully driving cock sunk deeply between her thighs.

Suddenly the girl's back arched and she pushed upward with a frightening power that almost threw the old man out of the saddle. "Ooooh God... I'm coming again, Derek, love me, fuck me harder... fuck fuck your big... cock... fuck, oh, Derek... Oh, God... I'm coming." With a deep-throated groan: her body began convulsing in lewd untamed pleasure. Hot wet cum spurted from the throbbing passage, its sticky warmth flowing down the crevice created by her buttocks; the viscous fluid inundated her anus — bringing an appreciative sigh from McAlister. She jerked about frantically, as though she were suffering some sort of seizure. She clawed at the old man's back; her legs pumped against him as she sought to drive him in deeper. Drymuir's face was taut as he sought his own release; he rammed his reaming cock forward with all his strength. His body drooped down heavily on her, mashing her full ripe tits against his own hairy chest. His long, punishing strokes moved violently in and out of the steaming passage that was now wet and slippery from the girl's continuing climax. Abruptly, he could feel the orgasm starting, as if a gunpowder trail had been lit that led to the powder-store of his tortured balls. Then the accumulated semen exploded violently and his prick throbbed once, twice... and began to spurt.

"Oh, yes, darling. Come in me... come all the way inside of me, Derek." Amanda chanted as her head rolled laxly from side to side and she frantically pumped her vagina up and down the long spurting rod of flesh in an effort to drain it of everything.

Lord Drymuir felt the hot slippery walls of her cunt sucking hungrily at his cock until there was nothing left in him, and his hardened organ began to deflate.

The girl lay back full-length in bed, with his prick still buried inside her. "That was wonderful, darling," she said, huskily. Her eyes closed in weary pleasure.

Lord Drymuir slowly pulled his slippery penis from the girl. She moaned as though reluctant to have it leave her body.

McAlister, who had been becoming increasingly impatient, took a last closeup as the prick slowly slid out of her battered cunt followed by a rivulet of white spunk. He could see the girl's wet matted pubic hair — like black moss hanging over a peaceful river bank — glistening on either side of her vagina. The insides of her milky white thighs were smeared with the cum from both of their bodies. The open crevice of her ass was completely wet from it, and McAlister knew he could stand the sight no longer. If ever a woman was lubricated and ready for sodomizing this one was. He already knew how it would feel — hot, tight... oh, so very tight! — and beautiful.

"Hurry," he grunted to Lord Drymuir, as be dropped his trousers. His own cock, proud, stiff and tall as the caber that strong men tossed at the local Highland games, was more than ready.

Lord Drymuir wearily dried his wet penis on his underpants and pulled on his trousers. A moment later he was standing behind the tripod camera. "All right," he said. "Ready any time you are, John."

McAlister said to the girl, "Amanda... I am your husband, Derek. Say something to me."

The girl scrunched herself deeper into the bed and mumbled hypnotically, "Derek, darling, I love you."

McAlister said, "Amanda, darling, don't you want to repay your husband for the pleasure I just gave you? It would be nice if you sucked on my cock again."

There was no hesitation this time. Amanda turned her head and opened her mouth. There was a flash of light and Lord Drymuir nodded.

"Now, Amanda, I'm going to make love to you in a new and excitingly different way. Get on your hands and knees... that's right, and spread your legs out wide."

The girl did as she was told. Lord Drymuir moved in with the closeup camera. McAlister used both thumbs to part the smooth white cheeks of her tender young buttocks and reveal the quivering, puckered little brown circle no larger than a florin. Really, he thought in ecstasy, it looks like an oval of tiny pink lips. He rubbed his prick in the crevice, lubricating it from Lord Drymuir and the girl's cum. The girl winced when McAlister inserted his middle finger into the opening. He moved it in and out, and around and around. The girl moaned in acute discomfort when a second finger joined the first. Then McAlister could stand it no longer: placing the tip of his hardened cock against her tight, puckered arsehole, he plunged forward...

The photograph was taken just as the head of McAlister's cock disappeared through the resisting ring of anal muscle. Lord Drymuir continued to shoot pictures as McAlister gleefully pounded his prick into the tube of her rectum and until her groans of pain became mewls of pleasure and surprise and finally of screaming release of a third orgasm as her helplessly impaled body reacted like a bitch in heat to the unnatural invasion of her bowels.

***

Downstairs, the clock struck twice. Lord Drymuir helped McAlister change the badly stained and wet linens on the bed, as the girl stood blank-eyed and stiff near the closet.

"Get back in bed, Amanda," McAlister ordered.

The girl walked like a zombie across the room and climbed into bed.

McAlister pulled the covers up to her shoulders, then began intoning, "You are sleepy... sleep. When you wake up tomorrow morning at nine o'clock you won't remember that we were here. Anything you will recall will be simply a dream about your husband. Do you understand? You have been dreaming about Derek fucking you. Say it!"

"I... have... been dreaming... about Derek... fucking... me."

"Yes, you have been dreaming. You are sleepy. Your eyes are so heavy that you cannot open them. You are sleepy... so very sleepy."

The girl slumbered peacefully.

McAlister glanced at his watch. "Two fifteen. Almost time for 'Derek dear' to wake up next to my wife. Care to bring your camera along and take candid snapshots, Cousin?"

"Wouldn't miss it for the world, old boy," Lord Drymuir laughed lewdly. "Wouldn't miss it for the world. If his John Thomas reacts half as well as his wife's hot little cunt, it should be quite a show." He clapped his hands together in eagerness. "I can hardly wait until tomorrow afternoon when we show that arrogant little bitch our 'honeymoon snaps'. How superb! How simply delightful! She'll come crawling to me then. Oh, she'll do anything. Anything!" he gleefully repeated. "And she'll do it fully conscious!"

The two men were still chuckling as they walked the darkened corridors of the castle. When they reached the East wing, McAlister pulled down on the handle of a sword on a suit of knight's armour. The hidden door swung silently open to reveal a well-lighted passageway. Two minutes later, they were seated in comfortable armchairs and drinking whiskey and sodas, as they watched — through the large pane of one-way glass — a young man slowly beginning to awaken next to a voluptuous nude woman who looked up directly at them and winked conspiratorially. Then her face changed. She rubbed her eyes to look as if she had been weeping, and when the boy was fully awake, she sobbed, "You beast, you. How could you... after we had offered you the hospitality of the castle... to cruelly rape me... Oh, Derek! And I was beginning to be so fond of you. What will poor Amanda think...?"

***

The following afternoon, a bewildered and ashamed Amanda "crawled" for her pictures, and then learned that she must continue to be nice for as long as McAlister and Lord Drymuir and their assorted friends decreed. Only then would she receive the negatives. That evening, she chose a third, unspoken, option, by leaping from the window of the castle's highest room and falling to her death on the jagged rocks some eighty feet below.

As John McAlister's wife, Mary, tried to console the weeping husband, the joint-owners of Castle Strathblane shook their heads. This time it had gone too far. They were lucky that the girl had a history of mental instability and suicide attempts.

CHAPTER ONE

The young girl – fifteen, freckled-faced, and with a surprisingly mature body for one her age – was dressed in skin-tight white shorts and was braless beneath her powder blue blouse. She lay crosswise on the bed, and stared up at an older girl who was standing before a mirror and running a comb through long blonde hair.

"But aren't you excited?" Cindy asked, shivering in vicarious enjoyment. "I mean... I would be! After all, your wedding is only two days away, and then you and Bill go to that groovy castle place in Scotland for your honeymoon. Why, you must be thrilled!"

"Of course I am, silly." Jenny's voice was patient with her cousin. "I'm happy and excited. But I'm also calm." That last statement was a lie, but Cindy couldn't know it. The younger girl couldn't see the turmoil Jenny felt, the oppressive feeling of apprehension that bordered on fear.

"It must be wonderful to be really in love and be old enough to get married... and wake up in bed next to your husband." Cindy put a hand to her mouth and giggled. "I mean my husband. If I had a husband."

"Cindy?" Jenny's voice had just a bit of shock in it; she gazed in mock severity at the girl and began weaving a thick braid into her hair.

Cindy's face was cupped in her hands; elbows were planted on the bedspread. The girl obviously decided to throw all caution to the winds with her next remark. "Well, isn't a bed better than a back seat?"

"Cindy!" Jenny threw down the comb and spun around to face the girl. "What are you talking about?"

"What else? Sex?"

Cindy had the bit in her teeth and was not to be denied. She abruptly sat up and curled her bare legs beneath her – sitting buddha-like on the bed. "If I tell you something, will you keep it a secret?"

"I don't want to hear it," Jenny said, emphatically. She was pretty sure of the drift of the conversation; this was nothing to discuss with a girl only fifteen. She hadn't even talked to her mother about it, even though the older woman had hinted broadly that they must have a conversation before the wedding.

Cindy looked toward the closed door of the bedroom as if suspecting someone were lurking outside at the keyhole. Then she lowered her voice and said, "I know you won't snitch." She grinned conspiratorially. "I'm not a virgin, you know."

The news momentarily shocked Jenny, although if she were really honest with herself, the information did not come as a surprise. Cindy showed all the signs of becoming a swinger, and she already had the build of a 22-year-old bikini model.

The girl continued almost proudly, "I haven't been one for almost a year. It was Dan Draper. After the final football game last October... after he was appointed head cheerleader. We had a bottle of beer and it made me dizzy, and then he... began feeling me. And, ah... asked me to feel him. Then he got in the backseat of his car and... ah..."

"I don't want to hear another word." Jenny's voice brooked no disobedience. "Not another word!" She shook her head in dismay. "I'm shocked at you, Cindy, really shocked. You're either fibbing or you just blithely gave away your virginity. Just like that," she snapped her fingers. "Just like you were giving away old clothes or something. I think you'd have more respect for yourself."

Cindy merely shrugged and her breasts jiggled with the motion. She replied, somewhat defiantly, "It was fun. It felt good. And I've let him do it five other times, too. We're going steady. We love each other. And everyone in school does it. Why not?"

"Why not? Well, I'll tell you why not. What does a fifteen year old know about love? What if your parents found out? What if the police discovered you and Dan in the back seat when you were... you were? What if you get pregnant as a result of it?"

Cindy snorted. "Oh, poo! I won't get pregnant. I'm not that dumb. Why, I wouldn't have let him do it the first time if he hadn't been wearing a rubber."

Jenny held up both hands commandingly. "I said before I don't want to hear anymore. I mean it."

The younger girl shrugged again. "Okay. Okay." She critically inspected Jenny, then cocked her head to one side and bit her lower lip in indecision. "You're a cool chick... real cool. But I wouldn't be surprised if you're still a virgin, even though Bill looks to me like he's the impatient type. He's probably snorting and pawing the stable floor." She wiggled her eyebrows suggestively.

Jenny strode to the door and angrily opened it. "Out!," she commanded.

Cindy insolently got up from the bed and stuck her feet into her sandals. Smirking knowingly, she walked across the room and stopped in the archway of the door. "I wouldn't have believed it – a girl as beautiful, as well built as you, a girl who has been engaged for over a year – still a virgin. Like wow!"

"Yes, damnit. I am still a virgin... and I am proud of it. Not that it's any of your business."

Cindy held out her hands beseechingly, "Okay... okay. Don't get mad. I was just curious. I never have seen a 20-year-old virgin before." She was grinning impudently as Jenny closed the door in her face.

Impertinent little snip, Jenny thought: My God, what are these high school kids coming to? She knew Cindy wasn't putting her on; the girl was telling the truth about Dan. A moment later, though Jenny's inherent common sense took over and she realized that only a strong will power had kept her, too, from losing her virginity. Cindy had been right about Bill, he was the 'impatient' type... but he was also understanding. He had proved that time and time again.

She and Bill had gone steady for almost two years before their engagement; and they had been engaged for almost twelve months now. While they were going steady, they had necked — some really passionate kissing had come about, but when Bill had begun fumbling for her breasts, she had managed to stop him each time. Since their engagement was announced and she received her ring, there had been some petting — at least on his part. She had permitted him the possession of her breasts and, three or four times, he had been allowed to touch that sacred area which would be completely his only after the marriage ceremony. Jenny had been forced to put a stop to his eager odysseys down there because of an underlying fear that she, herself, would lose all control. It did feel wonderful; that, at least, she could admit. Unfortunately, after these episodes, she would lie awake all night feeling the restless pounding of her heart being echoed deep within her womb. One night – for the first and only time – the throbbing had become so painfully intense that she had touched herself there with one finger. She moved it cautiously, and her lonely vagina cried out in ecstasy. A second finger joined the first, the two of them gently rubbing back and forth on the slit, now slick with her juices. The motions had become less tender – more rapid! She had continued this for almost fifteen minutes, but aside from her vagina becoming too tender to touch, nothing happened. She hadn't even come close to that elusive realm of physical release mentioned in various books. She tossed and turned all night – sleeping fitfully. The next morning she awakened to a deep sense of shame – a feeling that still came back with the full force of its guilty intensity each time she thought about it.

But now all that is past, she thought, as she finished braiding her hair. A moment later, she slipped on a green cardigan sweater to match her muted green-plaid mini-skirt, and started downstairs. Cindy, bright-eyed and undaunted, met her at the landing. "Like, wow! You're really getting some groovy loot," she said. "There must be a couple of tons of crap in there."

Jenny laughed in spite of herself, "Cindy, you are hopeless."

"Come on, let's see the stuff that came this morning." Cindy eagerly led the way to the living room where the already opened wedding gifts were piled atop each table as though they were luxury items on display in a small department store. Other gifts – unopened – were stacked on the floor. Cindy picked up one and shook it. "Try this one – from the Wilsons."

It was impossible not to laugh at the girl: she was as excited as a four year old under a Christmas tree. Jenny cautiously unwrapped the gift, taking care not to ruin the white satin ribbon, and saving the paper.

"Holy Donovan! A Waring blender – now, that's neat!" Cindy's exuberance was contagious. She grinned and affectionately put her arms around her cousin. "Come on," she said, "you can help me open them. But keep the ribbon, and the paper... and the boxes. And don't get the cards mixed up. Better write down what the gift is on each of the cards, so I can write thank-you letters later."

The two girls had been working almost an hour opening and recording the new gifts when the telephone rang.

Jenny, thinking it was Bill, answered it on the second ring.

"Jenny... this is Maria Dellacosta. Your gown's ready for final fitting. When can you try it on?"

"I'll come right over... if that's convenient for you."

"Come ahead, dear. I think you're going to be very pleased with it."

"Oh, I'm sure I will be," Jenny said ecstatically; then, as the doorbell rang, she shouted over her shoulder, "Cindy, get that, will you?"

"Be sure and bring the undergarments you're going to wear at the wedding," Mrs. Dellacosta added. "We want the gown to be just right."

"I'll be there in about five minutes." Jenny said, hanging up, and looking toward the door where the deliveryman from Kravitt's Department Store and Cindy were both carrying in additional gifts. Three different trips were made between the front door and the truck. Jenny signed the delivery slips while Cindy was busy counting and shaking packages.

"Golly, seventeen more gifts... and this one weighs about thirty pounds," Cindy's excited voice reported. "Shall we open them?"

"I can't right now. Mrs. Dellacosta wants to do the final fitting." Jenny saw the disappointed look on the girl's face. "Hey, why not come along to Mrs. Dellacosta's with me?"

"Oh... I'd like to, but Dan and I are going swimming. He's picking me up here in about twenty minutes or so. How long will you be? Will you be back before he comes?"

"I doubt it. The fitting probably will take at least an hour."

Cindy looked down at the rug and traced an abstract pattern with her big toe. "I don't suppose you'll change your mind about the hayride tonight?" she asked hopefully. "Dan and I wouldn't bother anyone. Honest. I promise!"

"I'm sorry, chicken. No. There will be liquor and, besides, everyone there will be in their twenties. We'll be just a bunch of old fogeys."

"Okay... if you don't want us."

"Look," Jenny said in an effort to make the girl feel better, "I'll save some packages for you to open tomorrow. Okay?"

"Ummm... I suppose so." It was said listlessly.

Jenny picked up her purse. "I've got to go. Be sure and lock up before you leave."

Five minutes later, Jenny was in a dressing room at Mrs. Dellacosta's. She quickly slipped on the blue lacy garter belt and her hose. "Now, dear, lift your hands straight up," Mrs. Dellacosta ordered. "No quick moves; the gown is just tacked. We don't want it falling apart." Jenny felt the rich silk garment slip down over her arms and bead. She looked at herself in the mirror. The gown clung to her like a second skin. Mrs. Dellacosta zipped up the long zipper in back then stood away to inspect her work. "Beautiful. Just beautiful!" Mrs. Dellacosta's face beamed over Jenny's shoulder in the mirror. "You like?" she asked, fitting a veil over Jenny's blonde hair.

"Oh, yes!" the girl answered sincerely. "It's... it's just..." She closed her eyes, unable to think of the appropriate phrase. It is so beautiful, she thought; Bill will love me in it.

The older woman smiled in understanding. "Well, that's all then. We'll sew it up this afternoon; I'll deliver it on Sunday around one."

"You mean... that's all? Nothing more for me to do?"

"Nothing," she said airily. "All you have to do is step into it Sunday at three, and then walk down the aisle."

Mrs. Dellacosta helped her out of the gown, and Jenny dressed again in her green sweater and plaid skirt. She glanced at her watch and was surprised to see that only ten minutes had elapsed. "Maybe Cindy will get to open some more packages after all," she said to herself.

It was a pleasant day, Jenny noted, as she walked the two blocks back to her home. Jenny felt like skipping, and she did... for a second or two until she remembered to be ladylike. She hoped the clear warm weather would hold until Sunday at least. She hoped it would be nice weather in Scotland. She hoped so many things, "But mainly I hope Bill and I will be happy together." She was humming a tune when she turned the corner and saw Dan's car in the driveway. Her step faltered; abruptly she remembered Cindy's candid confession about being intimate with the cheerleader. The boy was only sixteen, he might even be fifteen – not yet handsome, but fairly good-looking, with a pleasing personality. He had a kind of poise; Cindy had undoubtedly helped to bring part of that about. During the spring semester, he played shortstop on the high school baseball team – was too small of stature and build for football – and had earned his letter. Cindy and he made a rather attractive couple of teenagers, Jenny thought. Still, though, they were teenagers and should not have been physically intimate.

Knowing what she did, Jenny was sure that she would be unable to hide her mixed emotions if she faced the boy, so she walked around the side of the house and came quietly in the back way. She had planned to stay in the kitchen until he and Cindy left to go swimming. Obviously, they would have to be leaving in a minute or two.

The house was quiet – too quiet, she thought. Surely the young couple had left. For a moment, Jenny deliberated calling Cindy's name, then decided she would just walk in unannounced. After all, it was her home! Jenny left the kitchen and went through the alcove next to the living room. She was about to slide the doors open when she heard what sounded like a low cry of pain. Puzzled, she peered through the crack and then froze in shock and amazement. There, stretched out full length on the couch, were Dan and Cindy. The girl's white gym shorts had been unzipped and – together with her white cotton panties – were down about her knees. Her blouse was open all the way, and Dan's mouth was glued to her right breast. Even as Jenny watched Cindy groaned again – and Jenny realized it was not a cry of pain, but of delight. The boy's middle finger was sawing away in maniacal fury at the junction of Cindy's widely outspread legs. Her young pelvis was moving up and down in an effort to capture and hold on to the elusive digit. From her vantage point, Jenny could even see the engorged pink clitoris as large as a kidney bean.

Jenny knew she should go away – go back to the kitchen – and perhaps slam a door as if she had just entered. Then she could call out Cindy's name; that would give the boy and girl a chance to get into their clothes. But then she also knew that she wouldn't be able to face either one of them after what she was viewing now. Her attention snapped back to the front room as Cindy arched her back up off the sofa and began to pant hoarsely. "I'm coming, Dan," she cried once, then fell back, her face twisted in a lewd expression of delight and her legs beating against the leather couch.

After her movements had slowed, Dan took his finger away and lifted his mouth from her breast. He slid one knee over her thigh, as he began fumbling with his zipper. "Put it in for me, huh?" he requested.

"No! I told you no." Cindy said. In spite of the fact that her eyes were closed in satiation, there was no mistaking her adamant tone of voice.

"Please!" It was a frantic plea from the boy.

Cindy sighed in exasperation and opened her eyes. "I told you before you started messing around. It's the dangerous time of the month for me, and even if it wasn't, you'd still have to have protection. You know that!"

"Oh, God. I'm dying," the boy wailed.

Cindy sat up. She had a very patient expression on her face. "Lie on your back," she ordered, and turned on her side to give him more room.

Dan did as he was told. She suddenly realized that Cindy knew exactly what to do... had probably done this many times before. Even as she watched, Cindy expertly unfastened the boy's belt, undid the waistband hook, and then unzipped the trousers. His jockey shorts were bulging. Cindy's hand slipped in the opening and withdrew the penis.

She was frozen; she couldn't have moved now even if the house had been hit by a meteor. She had never seen anything like this before, although she knew it must happen all the time between some boys and girls. It had almost happened with her and Bill. That didn't change the situation; it was still lewd, dangerous, and wicked. Cindy's hand encircled the virile instrument at a point just below the head of the organ. She began moving her hand up and down, up and down. Dan lay back with a blissful look on his face, his eyelids fluttering, and his breath coming rapidly.

"Let me know," Cindy said.

"Yeah... yeah..." it was a hoarse grunt.

Less than thirty seconds later, Dan raised his buttocks off the couch and his face twisted in a grimace, "Ahh... ohhh," was all he said, but the communication was obviously effective for Cindy quickly used her other hand to pull up the jockey shorts just as the first white spurts of the boy's sperm came flooding through the subterranean channels of his penis. Cindy continued to stroke him – more gently now – and on her face was an unfathomable look that might have been either pleasure or satisfaction. Finally her hand motions stopped. She grinned down at the boy. "Feel better, sugar?" Jenny asked softly.

"Ummm. God, yes," Dan sighed. "It's not as good as the real thing – like fucking inside of you... but it's better than nothing."

Cindy laughed, "And better than doing it yourself?"

"Hey now. I don't..."

"You do," and she hit him playfully, "doesn't

everyone?"

After a moment, Cindy brought her hand out from beneath his jockey shorts. Jenny could see the hand was all wet; it glistened in the reflected light. Cindy calmly wiped her hand on the tail of his tee shirt. Dan turned his head toward her; Cindy's breast was only three inches away from his mouth. He parted his lips, his tongue came out and licked the erect brown nipple.

With a look of rapture on her face, Cindy put her hand behind his head and pulled him closer to her. His mouth opened all the way as he seemingly attempted to devour the entire breast. "Ummm... that's wonderful." Then, abruptly, she pulled away from him and was very businesslike. "That's enough," she said in mock sternness. "We'd better get going. Jenny will be back in a few minutes. Come on... get up, lazy." She prodded him with her knee.

Reluctantly, Dan stood up and faced the alcove door behind which Jenny was hiding. His levis were down around his knees, and he stood straddle-legged to keep them from slipping down any further. In an attempt to straighten out his sopping wet jockey shorts, he was forced to lower them to about mid-thigh. Jenny saw his cum-covered penis, flaccid now and only about two and a half inches long. He used the lower part of his tee shirt to dry it, and the vigorous drying motions started the organ swelling and elongating again. Cindy unconcernedly got off the couch, and Jenny was able to see sparse young triangle of pubic hair before the white cotton panties and tight white gym shorts hid it from sight. Casually, the girl buttoned up her blouse, all the while smiling affectionately at the boy. A moment later, arm in arm and giggling, they left; this was followed by the sound of Dan's car starting up.

Jenny suddenly realized that she was debilitated – so weak that her legs were almost unable to support her weight. She felt shame at having acted as a Peeping Tom, but more than that, she could feel a sense of forbidden excitement that raged like a wild fire in her own loins and brought a hot fevered dampness between her thighs. For a moment, when the boy and girl had been petting, it seemed almost as if Jenny herself were being fondled. Woodenly, she slid the door open and walked to the couch. She reached out one trembling hand and touched the leather. No, it hadn't been a dream. The leather was still warm from the heat of their bodies and, in one place where Cindy had lain with her bare buttocks pressed against the sofa. She could feel dampness where the girl's love juices had flowed down between her legs to the couch itself.

She sat down and thought about what she had seen. The performance of the two teenagers was wrong. Not only wrong, but sinful and dangerous. Yet, on the other hand, it had seemed such a natural thing and so very enjoyable! She had no doubt that the real act of sexual intercourse between Dan and Cindy would be just as natural – accepted just as calmly. And her thoughts moved on to her relationship with Bill. When she permitted Bill to fondle her, she had known excitement... at least for a few happy, beautiful moments. Always, though, she had become frightened as she felt her senses drifting away leaving her body helpless to any onslaught. And so, she had tightened up each time. As for touching Bill's penis... no matter how much Bill wanted her to caress him, she couldn't bring herself to do it. His male organ frightened her. Even though she had never seen it, she knew it was much, much larger than Dan's.

Jenny picked up a wedding gift. "Everything will be much better after the wedding," she said aloud, and felt immediate depression because she was pretty sure it wouldn't be that much better. She forced herself to grin and began ripping the paper off the package. "I am just having pre-nuptial jitters. Every bride has them. Don't they?" And she laughed humourlessly with the realization she was talking to herself. More than once during the next hour her eyes fastened on the couch, and she found herself wondering what it would be like if she and Bill...

Five hours later, when Bill came to pick her up for the traditional "final date" before marriage, the combination of perturbation and forbidden excitement still racked her body. She met Bill at the door, threw her arms around his waist, and kissed him warmly. As she pressed her body in close to him, she could sense his surprise at her uninhibited welcome. Her mouth opened to receive his tongue and her own tongue quivered and played effusively with his.

Bill, delighted with the greeting, drew back and asked, "What gives here?"

"I can kiss my husband-to-be, can't I?" she said, grinning in what she hoped was a wicked manner.

"Anytime, baby. Anyway!" They clenched again, then drew quickly apart as Jenny's mother banged a door at the top of the stairs and came down.

"Good evening, William," she said, primly, not smiling.

"Hello, Mrs. Jones. How are you this evening?"

"Not very well, thank you. I have a headache." Silence settled over the group. Jenny finally broke it by taking Bill's arm and saying, "Don't wait up, Mother. It'll probably be after midnight before we get back from the hayride."

Mrs. Jones stared at Jenny, then nodded. "Have a good time," she said, and it was obvious the statement was made perfunctorily.

Bill opened the door for Jenny and led the way to his side of the convertible. She slid in, showing more thigh than she usually showed, and didn't bother to pull down her skirt when Bill got behind the wheel. His mind was on something else, it seemed. "Brrr," he said, shivering as though he were freezing. "It was a bit cold in there tonight."

Jenny quickly put her hand over his. "Mother means well."

"Sure," he answered, starting the car and backing out of the driveway. "Just like last week when I told her to cheer up; that she wasn't losing a, daughter, she was gaining a son. She looked at me like I was something that had crawled out of the apple pie and said, 'I am losing a daughter.'"

"Everything will be all right," Jenny said, moving over until her hip was touching his.

Bill looked down at her legs and breasts, grinned, and said, "Everything is perfect already."

She beamed and replied, "Thank you, kind sir," and felt the happiness well up in her.

Bill drove quickly – surely – driving with one hand, with his other arm around her shoulders. His tape deck was playing something soft – something for people in love. Neither of them spoke as they drove out of town, heading toward the farm where the hay wagon ride was to originate. They were the last to arrive. Other couples were already in the wagon, and shouting impatiently for the evening to begin. Several bottles of hard liquor were in evidence, being passed around to be drunk straight. Jenny had a mouthful of straight bourbon and coughed as it burned its way down her throat to her empty stomach.

Someone began singing as the two horses pulled the wagon across the countryside. With the coming of darkness, the various couples began snuggling down into the sweet – smelling hay. There were muffled giggles from the girls and occasional barks of laughter from the boys. Jenny knew all of the others on the ride – most of them had been friends since kindergarten. They were a nice bunch of kids, she thought.

Bill pulled her down deeper into the hay, and she found herself almost buried in it, and lying full-length and pressed against him. The image of Dan and Cindy came to her at once, but she forced it out of her mind by asking, "Happy?"

"Uh-huh. You?"

In reply, she kissed him and found his mouth partially open: without volition, her tongue swam into his mouth. He savagely returned the kiss, and the excitement Jenny had felt earlier was rekindled. Now Bill's hands cautiously touched her breasts. Even through the sweater, blouse, slip and brassiere, she had felt the electricity between them.

The spell was momentarily broken when from the other side of the wagon, Jo-Ann Porter, the pert little redhead who was to serve as bridesmaid on Sunday, said very loudly, "Rod Greene. You stop that. You just behave yourself. You hear?" The remark was followed by ribald laughter from all the boys, including Bill. Even the driver, a 70-year-old coloured man, doubled up in laughter.

A second later, Bill began kissing her again. Their two tongues sparred, and she felt his hands becoming more sure of themselves when she did not protest. Lying as they were, face to face, Jenny was also becoming very aware of the hard bulge beneath his trousers, which confessed his desire. She wanted to reach down there and caress him the way Cindy had caressed Dan; she was steeling herself to do it when his hands moved beneath her sweater and his knee moved between her thighs, separating them.

She made no effort to halt his fumbling efforts to unfasten the bra clasp, trusting him and herself.

His movements, concealed by the straw and the night, were successful. A delicious moment later, his bare hand was on her naked breast; his fingers played over the nipple and he lovingly squeezed the firm, full mound of flesh. Never before had it felt so delightful to her. His tongue had become imperative, his movements almost frantic. His hips buffeted against her pelvis. She found herself panting – wanting him to stop, yet deep inside wanting him to go ahead forever. She wanted him to kiss and bite her breasts the way Dan had with Cindy. She was only vaguely aware of the clopping of the horses' hooves and the murmuring sounds of other couples who had also buried themselves in the anonymity of the hay. No doubt everyone was necking furiously, she thought. Suddenly, the breath went right out of her body. With one unhesitating smooth motion, Bill's hand slid up her thigh, dug itself under the thin elastic leg band of her panties, and touched the hot, moist lips of her now fevered vagina. Oh, God! She had been dying for him to do this... and now she didn't want him to. Immediately she dropped her arm and tried to pull his hand away; she also attempted to move her mouth from his. She was helpless, so weak. She was almost beside herself as he began massaging the hot throbbing passage between her legs. Once, his thumb and forefinger tweaked her clitoris which was tingling sensuously and a shower of ecstasy sparked through her groin. He began using his other arm to force her hand down toward the awesome bulge in his pants. She could feel reason leaving her; it was insane. "No... no!" she cried aloud and struggled upright. No one noticed her.

Jenny saw him looking at her, wild-eyed and trembling. Finally he seemed to gain control of himself and nodded that it was safe to come back into his arms. She did so, and with a final little shudder, kissed him gently on the lips. The bulge in his trousers felt even larger now, and she could feel it beating like a second heart against her bare thigh.

She had almost decided she would do something about relieving him, when the driver shouted to someone, and Jenny heard Jo-Ann Porter's voice, "Hey, everybody, we're here!" The wagon made a half circle and stopped at the bank of a river. A huge bonfire was scattering sparks to the night. The smell of broiling steaks came on the wind. A keg of beer was tapped as one of the farm hands began playing a guitar. Dinner was followed by a round of singing as the bonfire slowly died down. One by one, the couples began drifting into the perimeter's darkness.

Jenny felt Bill's hand pulling her to her feet. Arm in arm they walked down the dark beach. They had almost reached the end of the sand bar when he suddenly stiffened and whispered, "Shhh. There's someone out there." Jenny could hear the muffled groans and something that sounded suspiciously like the sound of body slapping against body. "What is it?" she whispered, half-frightened, not knowing what lay out there in the darkness.

She saw Bill grin and he put his mouth against

her ear. "I think it's Jo-Ann Porter and Rod Greene. Come on, let's see."

Jenny held back. "That wouldn't be nice," she hissed. "We shouldn't."

"Come on," Bill insisted, and took her hand. "Be quiet."

They moved silently across the beach heading toward the little gully that separated the sand bar from the bank. Bill pulled her low to the ground in order to cut down their silhouette. They peered over the bank.

Jenny made an audible gasp, which was quickly shut off by Bill's hand over her mouth. Her eyes were wide in amazement. There, down below them, only about ten feet away, were two nude bodies. Jo-Ann Porter's naked white thighs were spread wide and jerking frantically in the air as Rod Greene lay heavily between them. She saw Rod's buttocks rise, revealing a huge white rod of glistening flesh in the moonlight; the rod was sunk deep between Jo-Ann's open thighs! Rod thrust it forward and the girl's naked sex rose to meet it in midair. She squealed out in delight. Faster, faster, the two bodies moved against each other. Jo-Ann's breath was coming in loud, short, puppy-dog-like pants and her movements were frantic. "Fuck me harder, harder... oh, yes..." Jo-Ann groaned then, with her face contorted in lascivious lust and passion, cried out, "I'm coming, Rod. Ah! Ahhh... aieeeee. I'm coming. Fuck harder!" She made one maddened thrust upward and then fell back on the sand, her body going into uncontrollable spasm, her legs pounding the ground. A moment later, Rod rammed forward and groaned out his own release, and the couple lay still; the only sound was their hoarse exhausted breathing and the slap-slap of water as the little silver waves broke softly upon the sandbar.

Jenny was only vaguely aware of Bill leading her away into the darkness. Well, now she'd seen it. She knew the word for it; Jo-Ann had been 'fucked', and Jo-Ann had used the word 'come' as her body went insane with lust... just as Cindy had screamed out she was 'coming.' And Jo-Ann had enjoyed it, had obviously been deliriously happy during it... and so had Cindy.

The sight had almost maddened her with a strange, unwelcome desire. She could feel her own awakening loins beginning to lubricate. Bill was pulling her firmly away from the bank towards the darker shadows by the bluff. Once, when she opened her mouth to say something, he held up his hand and silenced her. After they had gone about fifty yards, he stopped and pulled her body around toward him. They kissed. Jenny wasn't attempting to tease him; she, too, had a fire in her loins that cried out to be extinguished. She didn't know how to put out the fire or how it could be put out; that would be Bill's job. All she knew was that she was instinctively grinding her pelvis against that forbidden area where his trousers bulged. Instinct told her that when these two junctions were finally joined, the fire would blaze up in an all-devouring conflagration, explode, and then slowly die like a beautiful sunset.

Standing on tiptoe, abdomen wantonly pressed against him. Jenny suddenly felt Bill's sure hands sweep up under the short skirt and cup her thin panty-covered buttocks in his palms. A second later, his thumbs hooked over the elastic waistband and with one delicious motion, her panties, were pulled down over her hips. Bill fumbled with his zipper and then the long hard rod, which had been held captive for so long, was released. It pressed hotly against her naked belly, throbbing hungrily with each beat of his heart. Standing pelvis to pelvis, she felt his knees spread outward a bit to lower himself. Then the fevered cock was between her thighs.

"Bill," she moaned. "Please... no. We can't." That was what her lips said, but her body was screaming, "Oh, yes... now, right now, my darling. What difference does a day or two make now?" And so, without conscious volition, she flexed and unflexed her thigh muscles against his throbbing penis knowing by his moan of pleasure that she was instinctively doing the right thing.

Bill sawed his cock between her thighs; she could feel the hardness of it moving back and forth inside its sheath of hot thin skin.

His finger had begun to seek out the now moistened entrance to her womb and after a second he found it. He turned his hand palm up to cup the whole of her naked crotch in his hand and, at the same time, force her thighs apart. She hated to lose that wonderful contact between her upper legs and his penis, but she permitted him to spread her anyway. His fingers were moving like those of a sensuous harp player across her soft, wet vaginal lips. She wanted to cry out in delight. Never before had she ever felt anything so soul consuming. Her neck arched and she moved her face from side to side, her lips contorted and panting out over and over again, "No... no... no," and obviously – from her wanton actions – meaning, "Yes... yes... yes."

Bill was grinding his teeth and grunting softly as he moved his penis up and down the length of her thighs. She could feel some moisture there; she wondered if he had 'come'. He still was hard, still was moving... so obviously, she thought, he hadn't reached his climax. There was a moisture – a hot, slippery moisture – in her own vaginal split; the artesian springs of passion coming to life under his quivering rod.

"Jenny... please! I want you. Let me." He continued to buffet her thighs with his prick.

I can't let you, she thought, incapable of speaking through her own longing. I can't stop you... I won't stop you if you really try. His huge rod now had slipped up to the top of her thighs and its head pressed and quivered against her hungrily throbbing cunt lips. She cried silently, "Oh, how I want you to make love to me. Do it now!"; nothing escaped her lips though except a wild, hoarse panting of desire. For the first time in her life she felt as if something good was about to happen to her down there, between her legs. Her heart rejoiced. There was no fear this time, as there had been in the past.

No sudden withdrawal of her senses. If anything, her senses stayed right there and intensified. It was beautiful. It was wonderful. She wanted to cry out to him, "Take me... take me now, darling." When her fiancé began pushing her gently down toward the sand, she went willingly. Panting, she lay on her back, legs slightly spread, looking up unseeing at the starry sky and watching as Bill unfastened his trousers and dropped them. Then he was kneeling between her thighs, the heat of his bare hips and buttocks against her abdomen and legs.

"Be gentle," she moaned, as she felt the huge head of his prick pressing at the lips of her unprotected vagina. She lay there, the heat of the moment on her – wanting it beyond all other things, and ecstatically happy that the terror had finally left her.

Bill's tongue sought possession of her mouth, his weight descended upon her lower belly, and the first gentle probe of his cock slid lengthwise across her vaginal lips. She gave herself to the sensation; she could feel all reason leaving her body – replaced only by pure feeling. Bill lifted his buttocks back a bit in preparation for this first entry. The throbbing head of his great phallus touched her vaginal lips, pushed forward and separated the soft yielding pubic hair, and paused there beating, beating, beating. Now he withdrew the head, now he replaced it and this time pressed just a trifle deeper. Oh, God, she thought; it is so beautiful. She could feel her vaginal lubricant oozing around the head of his cock. Now she wanted it deeper. Instinctively, she had reached down there to caress his balls when – with a terrifying suddenness – the breathless moment was shattered by the loud shrill tweet of a police whistle blown only a few yards away. And the sound of it caused Jenny's nerves to suddenly scream and react as though a stick of dynamite had exploded beneath her. Simultaneous with the whistle, which was the signal from the wagon driver that the evening was at an end, there was the sound of a giggle right above them, together with a muttered, "Ooops! Beg pardon." Jo-Ann and Rod were laughing as they backed away after stumbling over them in the darkness. "Didn't mean to break in," Rod's voice said, followed by Jo-Ann's hissed, "Shut up, Rod."

Jenny put her hands against Bill's chest and pushed him away. Frantically, she tugged at her skirt, attempting to pull it down and cover her naked loins. The beautiful moment had fled, and the way her nerves were screaming it was probable that it would not return for quite a long time. It was as though she were a child undergoing some sadistic psychological conditioning: reach out for a pretty flower and receive an electric shock upon contact.

Her nerve endings were all jangling like a hundred alarm systems being shorted out at once. She wanted to scream. Just as devastating was the embarrassment and humiliation that she felt. God, how cheap and vulgar she must have looked there with her legs spread out like a wanton whore. She covered her eyes and began sobbing quietly.

Bill, though, was not about to give up that easily. He sought to pull her skirt up again, but she jackknifed her knees beneath him and twisted on her side. "Don't!" she hissed, and it was an order not to be disobeyed. "I'm so embarrassed."

"God, we can't stop now," he groaned. "It doesn't matter if they saw us."

"It matters to me," and the sobs began coming more rapidly.

Bill angrily rolled over. "Oh, shit!" he said very loudly, and got to his feet, pulling up his trousers.

"I'm sorry," she wept. "I can't help it."

"Come on," he said, with little comfort in his voice, "Get up."

Trembling, Jenny stood and then feeling even more embarrassment, reached down and attempted to raise her panties; she heard them rip as her heel caught the elastic. Bill had his back to her. Why – oh why! – did everything go wrong all of a sudden. She had wanted him to make love to her – she needed to be made love to. He had even begun to make some penetration. And then that... that damned police whistle, together with Rod's crude laughter and Jo-Ann's knowing eyes. Contritely, she completed her dressing, and then said quietly, "Bill."

He refused to answer.

She sniffed. "Bill... I'm so sorry."

"Yeah, you acted like it," he mumbled.

"Well... I am."

"Okay," he said, his voice cold and distant, and not giving an inch. "You're sorry. I'm sorry. That doesn't make any difference to the condition I'm in right now – the same Goddamned condition I've been in ever since I met you. Don't be surprised if you hear tomorrow morning that I was arrested for raping someone on the street."

Jenny flared, "It's just as bad for me."

"I doubt it."

"What do you mean by that?" she asked.

"Forget it."

"No, I won't forget it. What did you mean?"

He turned finally and looked down at her. After a long moment, his shoulders slumped, and he sighed in exasperation. "You can turn it off. It's easy. Look at me, though. Just look!" He cupped his bulging trousers in one hand and clenched his fist tight around it. "What am I supposed to do with this? Christ! It hurts a man when he gets all set to make love and then nothing happens."

Jenny's retort was cut off by the sound of the police whistle again. Someone shouted their names, "Hey Bill... Jenny! Come on. Time to go!"

"Come on," Bill said, roughly grabbing her arm and leading the way toward the wagon. Jenny followed him docilely; she was thinking of what he said – about it hurting a man when nothing happens and he's ready. Cindy apparently knew the solution to that problem this afternoon with Dan. And at that moment, Jenny decided she would "relieve" Bill this way, if it would help him. He would have to make the first move, though; she couldn't bring herself to be that bold.

The ride back on the hay wagon was silent, and

the atmosphere painfully strained between the two of them. He made no effort to kiss or hold her. When they got back to the ranch yard, he had assisted her down from the wagon and then opened the door to the right side of the car – an obvious invitation to sit on her own side of the car. Not one single word was spoken during the short journey home. When he pulled into the doorway, he kept the motor running while he escorted her to the door.

Jenny's emotions were churning; she was torn between embarrassment, shame, and anger.

"Good night," he said, simply nodding his head, and again making no effort to kiss her.

All right, if that's the way you want to play it, to heck with you, Mister, Jenny thought. She forced herself to smile, though, and said, "Good night, Bill." She put her key into the lock, entered without looking at him, and closed the door behind her. She stood there, heart pounding, with her back pressed tightly against the door, until she heard the roar of his engine and the screech of his tires as he angrily departed.

"Jenny, darling, is that you?" Mrs. Jones's voice came from the living room.

She sighed, that was all she needed to make the evening a complete – an inquisition. "It's me, Mother."

"Come in here, please."

Jenny had no inclination to talk to anyone at the moment; all she wanted to do was go upstairs, take a hot shower, and go to bed with her own thoughts.

"Jenny? Are you all right?" Her mother's voice was insistent.

"Yes, Mother." Jenny took off her sweater and put it on the hallway bench. She glanced at her hair to make sure it was clean of hay and not too mussed, and checked her clothing for signs of disarray. Then she went into the living room where the older woman stood before the fireplace.

Mrs. Jones's eyes flickered over her daughter as if she were evaluating a stranger's honesty or trustworthiness. After a moment, she blinked and held a tightly wadded handkerchief up to her mouth.

Puzzled and alarmed, Jenny asked, "Mother? What's happened? What's wrong?"

Mrs. Jones seemed reluctant to speak. Then with big tears looming up in her eyes, she reached out for Jenny and said, "Oh, darling. I should have told you before, but it was go embarrassing for me." She sighed deeply, wiped her eyes with a lace handkerchief, and sniffed. "I just didn't want to embarrass you, too. But I can't avoid it any longer."

"What is it?"

"Sit down, dear." She motioned to the couch, then sat down beside her daughter. The older woman's face was flushing as she sought to put words to an obviously distasteful task. "I've never spoken to you about... about your marriage duties and marriage night. I must do so before you find out for yourself. This is something a mother must pass on to her daughter. It isn't something you will find in those horribly nasty dirty marriage manuals with their filthy pictures and diagrams... or those Communistic sex education classes they tried to put on in the high school. I'm so relieved that my woman's club was instrumental in getting rid of all that smut. After all, this is something that should be taught and discussed in the home."

She was appalled. This was the last thing she ever expected to hear from her usually reserved mother. The older woman was undergoing almost a Jekyll-Hyde transformation as she warmed to her subject. Earlier embarrassment had evaporated – being replaced by something akin to hatred and anger.

Mother said, "I think you know that men and women have different reproductive organs."

Jenny was amused in spite of herself, but she realized she must bite back her smile. She wondered what mother would say if daughter was to tell her that the first time she had ever seen – in living colour and stereophonic sound – a full-grown male's erect 'reproductive organ' had been that afternoon on the couch... that Mother was sitting on the exact spot where Cindy's 'reproductive organ' had damped the leather some 12 hours earlier... that Jenny's own 'reproductive organ' had been rubbed by Bill's 'reproductive organ' only an hour before.

Mother continued her lecture. "May I suggest that you use your... ah... reproductive organ as just that. Get pregnant right away, as soon as you can, then you won't be bothered by Bill. Sex, after all, is enjoyable only to men; it is something we women must bear with fortitude – no matter how distasteful."

Jenny swallowed, confused. "But, Mother," she protested, "sex is supposed to be beautiful between a husband and wife."

The older woman closed her eyes and shook her head. "Sex is only beautiful in that it leads to procreation. Remember the Bible: it says, 'Woman submit to your husband.' That word 'submit' means just that. Sex is a cross we women have to bear. Nothing is fair or equal about it. For example, on your wedding night, you will give your virginity to Bill. He will take it joyously. And what does that gift cause you? Not joy! Pain! Your hymen will be brutally ripped, the pain will be excruciating... and then you will begin to haemorrhage. I have even heard stories of women bleeding to death on their marriage bed. Once – you remember? – I broke my leg and the bone popped out of my skin?"

She nodded, remembering the afternoon when she was only five years old; she'd had nightmares for weeks after seeing the blood, the white bone, and hearing the sounds of her mother's screams.

"You remember how I finally passed out from the agony, and when they tried to move me I came to again, and how they had to give me morphine to ease the pain?"

Wide-eyed and wondering, Jenny said quietly, "Go on."

"Well, the pain that afternoon was nothing compared to the agony I suffered when your father took my virginity... even though he tried to be gentle. That, of course, was before he became an insensitive alcoholic brute." The older woman's eyes narrowed in recollection. "It was always painful. It hurt every time he insisted on my performing what he called 'marital obligations.'" She held up her hand as Jenny opened her mouth to speak. "Wait, don't interrupt. My mother suffered the same way, and her mother, and her mother's mother before her. Your poor Aunt Belinda! It is a fact of life you must learn to accept, and that is why I say to you, 'get pregnant as soon as you can'."

Jenny was slow putting her thoughts into words, but finally her feelings came tumbling out. "But... but don't most women enjoy making love with their husbands?"

"Whores! And don't disgrace that beautiful word 'love' by using it in that filthy context. 'Making love', indeed! 'Making war' would be more like it, for the woman is always defeated, degraded, and brutally subjected to all types of indignities. Can you image... (No, of course you can't, and pray God that you'll never have to!)... what it is like to have some foul breathed, wine-swilling, cigar stinking beast crawl like a spider over your naked body?" She shuddered from the thought of it; and Jenny – watching her mother's genuine horror – couldn't help thinking about what had been said.

Jenny was fairly sure that her mother was telling the truth – at least the truth as the older woman saw it. Perhaps there was an inherited physiological trait that had been passed on through the female genes in her mother's family. She had read and heard about such things. Perhaps it was painful! Maybe there was some almost insignificant anatomical or neurological difference in the female line of her family. And, abruptly, as the horrifying thought came to her, Jenny clutched the arm of the couch: Could the trait have been passed on to her? Would she know agony... instead of passionate enjoyment? Would she have experienced excruciating pain if Bill had continued his penetration?

Her mind was a maelstrom of confusion and fear. There were so many questions she wanted to ask now... and no one to answer them. Jenny wanted to ask if Mother had ever enjoyed a male's caresses and fondling, but such a question was embarrassing and at that moment almost senseless.

Then, almost as if reading her mind, her mother said, "I think almost all women enjoy 'sparking' with a man – the touch of his hand upon your arm," and the older woman blushed, "or a gentle kiss. The body responds, of course. But the act of sexual intercourse itself is degrading." A moment later she began speaking more rapidly – almost irrationally. "Remember what Saint Augustine wrote, 'Nothing is so much to be shunned as sex relations.' And remember what I said. Sexual intercourse should be used only for procreating the race. Birth is painful – horribly so – but the act of conception, of mindless copulation, is equally painful. Get pregnant, my darling, as soon as you can."

There was more of the same, but Jenny's mind could not absorb any more. Jenny knew her mother was wrong – terribly wrong. That statement about only "whores enjoying sex" was almost pathetic. Cindy certainly was no whore – nor was Jo-Ann. Then there was Cynthia and Donna, both of whom had been friends of Jenny's for almost all of her 22 years; both had married earlier this summer. They certainly weren't "whores", but they had made some ecstatic reports about what their husbands did to them in bed.

Long after she had gone upstairs, Jenny lay awake – unable to sleep. She gradually became more and more certain that her mother was telling the truth as she saw it. It was painful to Mother; it probably was agonizing... to Mother, to Mother's mother, and Aunt Belinda. If it was true, and Jenny had absolutely no reason to doubt it, then most probably the same thing was inherently wrong with her. It would be as agonizing for her as her ancestors once Bill made full penetration.

It was a family curse, her confused mind decided; a curse handed down from one female to another on her mother's side.

Down there – deep within her womb – she felt her vaginal muscles tighten. It was a though a lock had been put in place... a lock without a key... a lock that would keep Spring and Summer out forevermore.

CHAPTER TWO

Bill knew he was acting like an immature teenager when he burned rubber pulling away from Jenny's house. He had popped the clutch without thinking, his mind too full of anger and unhappiness to care about noise or wear and tear on the new car. His anger was directed against not only Jenny, but himself as well.

He realized Jenny wanted to keep her virginity intact until the wedding; that, at least was understandable. It was all right with him, too, as long as he could occasionally score with a college girl from out of town or one of the occasional hungry, but discreet older married women he met while working as sales manager in his father's imported automobile showrooms. The really big problem was that Jenny kept displaying these frustrating moments of willingness to go all the way... until she began getting up tight. She wasn't a prick tease; it seemed more like she was really scared.

He rubbed his cock through the material of his trousers. His balls were hurting again – the usual occurrence after a date with Jenny. "Jeez, we came so close tonight, and she was almost letting me," he said aloud, and then added, "that God-damned police whistle scared hell out of me, too. And Rod making with the wise cracks... that's all we needed..." Jenny had tightened up like quick-setting concrete the second she heard the whistle; it was almost as if she had suffered instant rigor mortis. Then something had seemed to have collapsed inside her when she realized there were voyeurs. That had been Rod's idea of a practical joke – butting in just at that moment.

Bill stopped his car at a traffic signal; when the light turned green, he raced another car away from the light, burning rubber for almost half a block. A black and white police car coming in the opposite direction blinked its headlights in warning at him, and Bill immediately slowed down. He watched in his rear view mirror, but the police car continued its patrol and did not turn around in pursuit.

When he turned off the Boulevard onto Main, he was surprised to see Rod Greene's sports car on the side of the road; its parking lights were blinking, and an irritable, cursing Rod had his head under the hood.

"What's wrong, pal?" Bill asked as he pulled alongside and stopped.

Rod looked up. "Oh, this son of a bitching oil line blew on me again. Third time this week. Christ, for two bits I'd drive the God-damned thing over the edge and dance a jig all the time it was sinking into sixty feet of water."

"You know where to come for a good new one."

Rod stuck out his tongue and made an obscene noise.

Bill laughed. "Anything I can do to help?"

"Not unless you've got three feet of quarter inch copper tubing?"

"'Fraid not. Can I call a garage for you?"

"Naw. The cops came by a few minutes ago and radioed for the auto club; but the tow truck is out on the highway with a wreck right now. They can't be here for another half hour or so."

"Okay... see you later then," Bill said, and put the car in gear.

"Hey, wait!" Rod came over to the side of the car, a troubled look on his face. "Say... ah... you could do me a favour."

"Sure, anything."

Rod nodded toward the front seat of his car. "Can you give her a lift home? Her old man's going to be raising all sorts of hell even now; another thirty minutes, he'll probably be waiting on the front porch with a shotgun."

For the first time, Bill saw Jo-Ann Porter peering at him from the dimness of the front seat. "Hi there," she said, brightly.

"Hello, Jo-Ann." Bill shrugged as he turned back to Rod. "Would you rather I stay with your car, and you take her home in mine?"

"Naw. I'm the only one who can sign the auto club slip. Besides, with an Honest John citizen like you bringing her home, her old man will have to believe that I actually did have car trouble this time."

"Right." Bill leaned across the seat and unlocked the door. "Come on Jo-Ann... got your bus transfer?"

Jo-Ann slid out of the driver's side of Rod's car, and her little mini-miniskirt crept up almost to her waist. From the position of her legs, it was difficult to tell if she were wearing panties or not. Rod paid no particular attention to her or her legs. "I'll call you tomorrow," he said, patting her shoulder, and then looking over at Bill, "Thanks."

"No sweat," Bill answered. "Want me to come back after I've dropped her off?"

Rod shook his head. "Not necessary. I'll manage." A moment later, he was lost to sight as Bill turned the corner.

Bill was all too aware of Jo-Ann's body next to him, even though she sat next to the opposite door. She'd made no effort to pull down her skirt when she got into the car. Her well-shaped thighs were really something to look at, he thought, and the proud upthrusting of her breasts beneath her sweater gave ample evidence that she had not bothered to put her bra back on after the beach episode... if, indeed, she had ever worn one at all. He'd be willing to bet that she wasn't wearing panties, either. These thoughts and remembrance of the beach scene brought stirring life to Bill's penis again. The vision of Jo-Ann being soundly fucked by Rod came back all too vividly. He knew he was tensing up, knew his prick was beginning to swell painfully again... knew also that Jo-Ann was aware of his tenseness. God, that's all he needed now – another hard on! And with Jo-Ann, one of Jenny's best friends.

It was she who spoke first, saying, "Look... I'm sorry we... Rod and I... ah... interrupted – intruded, tonight."

He shrugged. "It's okay. You really didn't see anything anyway, because nothing happened."

"I really didn't think so."

"What do you mean?"

Now she shrugged, and gave a knowing little smile. "You're too up tight. You'd be more relaxed... if something had happened."

"Is it that obvious?" Bill asked, mildly astonished at the girl's boldness.

Jo-Ann grinned. "You might say that it's obvious as hell." Without a warning, she reached over and touched the bulge in his trousers. "Like so." The contact created the same result in his loins as a match struck in a gasoline-vapoured chamber. She left her hand, not teasing him, not caressing... merely resting her fingers on the throbbing cloth lump created by his desire. Jo-Ann's eyes were locked on his face; the intensity of her glance was something he could feel. She seemed to be asking silent questions – and receiving silent answers. Bill was aware that he was driving very slowly now – the vehicle was barely moving, as a matter of fact. His breath caught with the next comment from the girl, "If we hadn't intruded, you wouldn't be uptight. Would you?"

Bill had to force the words out of his suddenly dry throat. "I guess not." He kept his eyes on the road.

"Then... I'm responsible in a way." She looked over her shoulder out the rear view window, then glanced ahead of them. "Keep driving," she ordered. She had some plan, obviously; her actions were unmistakable.

Through a haze of uncertainty and growing heat, Bill felt her hand leave his leg and begin fumbling with his belt. "Take a deep breath," Jo-Ann said. He did as instructed, and she quickly unfastened his waistband. A second later his zipper scraped, and her knowledgeable hand and fingers released his hot throbbing cock from the imprisoning confines of his shorts. He groaned deep in his throat as she stroked it a couple of times. "My... it's beautiful," she said, breathlessly. "So big! So hard!" She lovingly pumped it for a few seconds, then rolled it like a thick cigar between her fingers. The reflected light from the dashboard instruments showed her hand moving up and down on his long white prick. God, how he had wanted a girl to do that! It was almost more than he could stand. Already, even though only thirty or forty seconds had elapsed, he could feel the gathering thunderheads in his balls. The girl was an expert; she knew exactly what to do and how to do it. He groaned, and his breath began coming faster.

He was so caught up in the delicious sensation that Jo-Ann had to make the request twice.

"What?" he muttered, not really sure he comprehended.

"Move the seat back further," she repeated.

Bill mentally knew what was coming next. Eagerly, he reached down on his left for the seat release and pushed with his back. The seat slid all the way back. He was forced to drive with his arms almost straight out in front of him.

Jo-Ann glanced out the rear view window again – looked ahead at the vacant street – and ordered, "Just keep driving. Tell me if you see any cars coming from behind. Call this my wedding present to you." She bent forward and her hot lips slipped wetly down over the head of his bulging cock.

"Ahhhhhh," it was a moan of delight wrenched from his soul. Nothing had ever felt so beautiful before, or at least nothing recently. Her tongue flickered at the urethral opening and then ran maddening circles around the head. She had pursed out her lips so that her mouth felt like a soft hot clamping vaginal ring, wonderfully moistened. With her free hand, she reached down into his snorts and began gently squeezing his testicles in rhythm to her sucking movements. Up and down her mouth moved, gently bobbing like an oil pump pulling precious liquid from the subterranean depths. Bill was about to go out of his mind from the sensation. The girl had said to keep driving, but it was almost impossible to do that because of what he felt. He couldn't have been travelling more than three or four miles an hour when the girl, as if sensing his impending orgasm, began taking the cock deep into her throat. Faster, faster, faster her head moved until Bill could stand it no longer. He arched his back and raised his buttocks off the seat in an effort to jam it further down her throat. She took it all, and as the head of his prick began swelling to enormous size, Jenny started sucking voraciously, interspersing the vacuum with occasional little nibbles using her teeth against the trunk and head. The dash lights showed her lips being pulled out grotesquely as they clung to his white driving rod. He continued to push up to meet her, and she continued to take him. His mouth was swollen shut and long hoarse pants of breath whistled through it. His prick felt as though it weighed a ton – a ton of hot molten lava restlessly surging below the surface of a volcano. He knew he was on the verge of coming and felt he should prepare her but as her motions became more rapid and the suction increased, he suddenly knew it didn't matter. She obviously had done this before; she was an expert. The lava gathered, seethed and boiled. The eruption was imminent. Low guttural noises of delight came rumbling out of his throat. He was coming... coming... almost there. Almost. Now... Now! Now! The first hot spurts of sperm boiled out of his balls and screamed along the duct leading to the head of his cock. "Ahhhh... hahhhh... ohhhh!" His cry was meant to give her some warning, but the sound merely increased her frenzy. The hot cum roared out of his cock in great, smooth gushing quantities and she went on sucking furiously as he shot everything he had into her wonderfully warm, greedy mouth. And still he came, as weeks of pent up frustration and abstinence manifested themselves in almost half a cup of the viscous elixir of love.

She used her tongue to tease, her mouth and lips to suck, until his penis became less osseous and began to deflate. It was as though she felt it necessary to suck every last drop of lust from him. She continued to work until he was sure he was getting ready for another erection, and then she suddenly stopped.

Bill gave a mumbled sigh of happy release, and abruptly became aware that his car – lights on, motor running – was standing motionless right in the middle of the street. Jo-Ann withdrew her dripping lips from his cock, then kissed its head which was inflamed from her nibbling and smeared with her lipstick. She slithered up until she was enclosed in his arms. Then she kissed him wetly; her tongue darted and licked around his mouth. He could taste the alien taste – the taste of his own sperm in her mouth. Jo-Ann's face was slippery – glistening from his seminal juices and streaked with her lipstick. She scooted back over to her own side of the car, opened her purse, and carefully wiped her mouth with a Kleenex as he began driving again. He turned onto the street where she lived as she glanced over toward him, "Do I look presentable?"

He inspected her face, and nodded.

She smiled as he stopped in front of her house and started to get out of the car to open the door for her. "Don't bother," she said quickly and slid out. As her skirt flared up, he realized he had been right; she wasn't wearing panties, after all. The crack of her smooth young buttocks was a dark inviting line at the top of her white thighs.

Bill saw her father part the curtains and stare angrily out into the night.

"He's seen you," Jo-Ann said. "So now he'll believe the story about Rod's car." She grinned impishly at him as she closed the car door and leaned through the window, "Did you like my wedding gift?"

"The greatest."

Her laughter came floating through the cool night air and, as she turned to go up the walkway, she tossed back over her shoulder, "Make sure Jenny sends me a 'thank you' note." She was still laughing when the door closed behind her excessively wiggling little ass.

Relaxed and sleepy, and feeling only a minor pang of remorse at having betrayed Jenny with one of her best friends, Bill drove slowly homeward. He puzzled over the opposite sexual reactions of the two girls; there was all the difference in the world between them. Jenny was loving. She had moments of great warmth and tenderness that seemed to engulf him like a pleasant comforter on a cold night. Yet, she had very obvious sexual hang-ups. He knew – from the way she reacted when he caressed her – that she couldn't be frigid... at least not in the technical sense. She seemed more just frightened.

Jo-Ann was a different proposition. She was 'hot'; from the gossip among the fellows, Bill knew she fucked like a bunny and had been doing so since her freshman year in high school. She also had other talents in the sexual line, as she had just demonstrated! There were a lot of girls in the world like Jo-Ann; he had known a few himself before he became engaged to Jenny. Some of them already at 14 or 15 – were tramps, and that, he knew, was the kindest word for them. They pretended sexual excitement, they screwed, they bellowed, when they reached their pitiful little climaxes, but there was always something missing. Jo-Ann really couldn't be called a tramp. She considered sex as merely another adjunct to friendship, and thus she enjoyed a good fuck. When she got married, she would be the one who suggested husband swapping.

And Jenny? There was an untapped reservoir of passion in her; he could sense it. There was more power, more heat in her loins than in Jo-Ann's. But how to reach it: now that was another thing entirely.

As he drove into his own driveway, he thought sleepily: Maybe Jenny will change once she gets the wedding ring. He was sure she would, otherwise the marriage would never go. She wasn't at all like her mother – dour and dried up and seemingly hating men. At least... he prayed she wasn't like her mother.

As he got out of his car he felt the dampness of his shorts where the seminal juices had seeped after Jo-Ann had finished her ministrations. For a moment, he visualized Jenny doing that for him; such an act would be clear evidence that she had rid herself of some of the hang-ups.

And, abruptly, he had an erection – just as big and powerful... and painful, as earlier. The thought of Jenny doing that stayed with him even after he hopped into the shower and until he soaped his penis – running his slippery hands up and down its throbbing trunk. Then... feeling as foolish as a 15 year old... he soaped until his huge rod spat out its load against the tile walls of the shower stall. He watched, slack-jawed, as the cum ran down the tiles, and he thought: that's the last time I'll ever have to do that again...

CHAPTER THREE

Saturday passed in a whirlwind of activity for Jenny. The wedding rehearsal was scheduled for four-thirty in the afternoon; it was to be followed by a dinner for the bridesmaids and ushers. She felt awkward when she met Bill at the church that afternoon; she had planned to apologize to him, to hold him and have him hold her. Yet, the second she saw him, an unwanted thought boiled up in her mind: He is going to hurt me tomorrow night... I know it!

Bill, however, surprised her by apologizing for his short behaviour the night before. He seemed somehow different today – more relaxed and at ease. Abruptly, Jenny felt all her doubts dissipating. He was to be her husband; he would protect her. He would never hurt her on purpose.

And so the rehearsal passed, and Jenny was in a glow of happiness as she sat holding hands with him during the pre-wedding dinner, listening to the idle gossip and chatter of the other couples. When he kissed her goodnight at the front door, it was almost midnight. She responded warmly to him. "This will be the last time," Jenny said softly, her voice full of love.

"The last time what?"

"The last time you'll have to say 'goodnight' like

this." She knew her face was aflame as she said, boldly, "Tomorrow night you can whisper it before we go to sleep."

Then she was inside the house. The spell was broken immediately. Aunt Belinda, her mother's sister, was talking loudly in the front room. Her strident voice cut through the hallways like a scythe through thick grass. "I still say Jenny should have had a surgeon inject a local anaesthetic and then have the doctor cut her hymen. And maybe he could prescribe some sort of suppository she could insert each time before, which would deaden the pain. Why should she suffer needlessly?"

Mrs. Jones's whining voice came. "Oh, I tried to talk to her – to explain the disgusting thing that is going to happen... but she just sat there with a look on her face that said, 'Maybe it'll be different with me, Mother.' I just don't know what else to say to her; I don't want my only daughter to be hurt – to be degraded by some... some..." Her emotions obviously were getting the better of her.

There was a short pause before Aunt Belinda said, "Did you ever think... that Jenny might not be a virgin still?"

"Belinda! What a horrid thing to say!"

"Well?"

"Of course she is. I'm positive she hasn't cheapened herself that way."

There was another moment's silence, then Belinda said musingly, "Yes... I suppose you're right. She couldn't hide that from you. She would have been in pain for days when it happened. You would have known."

She could listen to no more. Why – oh why!
– did everyone have to conspire to ruin the most
beautiful moment of her life, she thought. Why?
Her mother and Aunt Belinda quibbling over
her virginity – discussing it as though Jenny were
some animal to be trained or doctored. Wasn't this
something between her and Bill? Was it anyone's
business but hers? She fought the impulse to run
in and shout at them, fought another impulse to
run up the stairs. Instead, she forced herself to
tip-toe quietly up to her bedroom. There, hanging
on the closet door like some ghostly figure mocking
her, was her bridal gown and veil. Jenny reached
out one trembling hand to the satin mesh. She
shuddered at the feel of it. Maybe, she thought in
sudden dismay, I should call the whole thing off
while there's still time. But she knew that it was
already too late.

When she heard Aunt Belinda and her mother's
querulous voice in the hall forty minutes later, she
pretended as if she were asleep. Her door opened
and the two women whispered in the darkness.
Her mother said, "She must have come in while we
were in the kitchen and not wanted to bother us."

Jenny felt someone standing next to the bed.
Then Aunt Belinda's soft voice said, "Look at her...
the poor child. Sleeping so innocently. For the last
time."

Her mother's sniffle was the only answer.

That night was spent with Jenny's body as rigid
as a railroad tie. She tried to sleep, but it was an

impossible task. When she glanced at the luminous hand of her watch, it was three o'clock, and she thought: Only twelve hours more.

When dawn finally came, Jenny was slumped dejectedly in a chair in front of the window, and was thinking that she still had nine hours in which to extricate herself from the trap of marriage. Sounds began in the kitchen a short time later as her mother and Aunt Belinda began the day's activities.

Breakfast – unwanted and tasteless – followed a shower, then Debbie arrived to do Jenny's hair. Jenny woodenly answered everyone's questions and made light conversation with the hairdresser. And during it all, she was thinking: Still three hours to call it off.

Then, with a flourish, Mrs. Dellacosta arrived to assist with the wedding gown; the first two bridesmaids followed her moments later.

And, abruptly, all of the sands had run out. It was time! Later, Jenny had absolutely no memory of being taken to the church; in many respects it was like a condemned man spending his last hours before taking that long last walk.

She heard organ music. She was walking – because someone had told her to begin walking and had nudged her. She saw a sea of smiling faces. She saw Bill's face, strained and smiling at her from the altar. She saw the bridesmaids in front of her scatter out like brilliantly coloured petals of flowers unfolding.

A face: the minister? "Do you accept this

man..."

Her nod and voice from a million miles off, "I do..."

"Do you accept this woman..."

And Bill's voice – hoarse – answering...

"I now pronounce you..." The strident roar of the organ, the brilliant blindness of the sunlight outside the chapel... the flash of the photographer's camera. The sting of thrown rice... the shouted congratulations and, from a couple of the junior high school kids who had been invited, "You'll be sorr-eeee." The reception line – a never-ending line of faces and kisses and mouths uttering words she couldn't comprehend. The cutting of the cake. Everything all a blur. Then Mrs. Dellacosta again – removing her gown – helping her dress in a new cerise tweed suit for travelling. A corsage being pinned to her coat.

Then Bill again... meeting her in the hallway of the second floor outside her bedrooms... holding her. A shout as the reception guests saw them. A mad dash down the front stairs to Bill's car all painted with signs. The car door slamming. People shouting gleefully. The sound of Bill's car starting, the screech of his tires as he attempted to elude the jokers who wanted to follow with horns blaring.

And the last – the very last – view of her house. Mother, and Aunt Belinda... like two dark accusing angels of doom, standing there silently – not waving... merely watching as the car drove off... an expression of grief on her mother's face...

She began weeping.

Bill patted her hand. "Okay?" he asked solicitously.

"Yes," she lied, through a muffled handkerchief, "I'm just so happy."

"This time tomorrow, we'll be in Scotland. And tomorrow night we'll be at the castle."

So full of dread was Jenny at the thought of this first night stretching in front of her that she didn't respond to his excitement.

"Just think of it," he continued eagerly. "Two weeks of doing nothing but lying in the sun and swimming all day and making loving all night."

"Yes, darling. It will be lots of fun," she said, not believing her own statement. The terror was beginning to boil up in her again.

Jenny became more tense – more silent – with each passing mile as they drew closer to the international airport hotel where they would stay tonight prior to boarding the plane early tomorrow morning. She tried to purge her mother's voice from her mind, but it came creeping back like a freezing bone – numbing fog. "Dear God," she prayed silently, "don't let me be like mother and Aunt Belinda. Don't make it repulsive or painful..." The dread, however, continued to permeate her every thought. She was close to tears when they checked into the hotel. The manager almost seemed to smirk at her when he led the way to their suite. Inside, there was a bottle of champagne on ice – courtesy of the owner – and inscribed, "To the honeymooners".

Almost frantic now with fear and nervousness,

Jenny pressed the manager to stay for a "toast." She didn't want to be left alone with Bill.

The manager merely smiled and said, "Oh, no! The champagne is just for the two of you lovebirds. Congratulations to you both. Have a good night, now!"

The door clicked behind him, and the nightmare began. Bill tried to take her in his arms, but she reflexively put both hands against his chest and pushed back. "What's wrong?" he asked genuinely perplexed.

"Nothing," she lied. "Just a splitting headache... I'll take an aspirin and be all right in a little while. Maybe you should take a shower?"

He looked concerned. "Is there anything I can do?"

"No. It'll go away. Take a shower."

Bill grinned in mistaken understanding. "Ah... I bet I know. You want to get rid of me while you change your clothes... and get into something more... ah... comfortable." He wiggled his eyebrows.

Jenny anxiously seized the remark. "Yes! Yes, darling!"

"All right. One shower coming up." Bill laughed and took off his coat. He opened the suitcase and brought out a new pair of blue silk pyjamas. He held them up for her inspection. "Pretty sexy, eh? Just wait until you see them on me." He kissed her passionately, then disappeared into the bathroom. A moment later, she heard the water being run and his voice raised in song.

Quickly, she removed her clothes and slipped into

the white peignoir purchased for the honeymoon. She caught a glimpse of herself in the mirror, and she blushed in shame. When she had tried the negligee on in the store she had been wearing panties under it. Now, however, it clearly showed the small dark triangle of her pubic hair and the brown nipples of her breasts. She opened the bed, climbed in, and pulled the covers up around her throat. Two minutes later Bill, somewhat flustered, came out of the bathroom. The reason for his chagrin was plainly evident; the front of his PJ bottom bulged out as though he had a huge banana protruding from between his legs.

"It must be something they put in the soap," he said, making a feeble joke.

Jenny did not laugh; she cringed deeper into the bed. Although she had felt his penis through his trousers before and although he had touched her with it before, never – not in her wildest imaginations – had she conceived it was as big as it appeared to be. Through the pyjamas it appeared to be at least twice as large as Dan's had been.

Now she knew what her mother had been trying to say; no woman's body could safely take that huge bulging staff. It would split her apart like a Parker House roll. She whimpered when Bill came alongside the bed. That... that thing was only inches away from her head as he turned out the light. Then she felt the covers being pulled back and Bill's body and his huge male organ of destruction pressing against her side. Without preliminaries, he kissed her – possessively at first and then with rapidly increasing passion. She responded only perfunctorily when he tried to shove his tongue down her throat.

Bill drew back from her. He leaned over on one elbow, "What's wrong, darling?" he asked.

"Nothing," the word was said so softly it was almost inaudible as she lay there transfixed with fright.

"Are you nervous?"

She leapt at the remark as though it were a life ring. Perhaps if she admitted to it, he would leave her alone tonight. So she said, "Yes... terribly nervous."

Bill laughed. "Well, then. We'll just have to take care of that nervousness. I've got just the thing to remove nervous strain. Leave everything to me." He kissed her neck and his hot wet tongue traced a design down to the top of her gown. She felt his hands pull down the straps of her gown, then he began caressing her bare breasts. She felt nothing except the fearing pounding within her heart. He bent forward and glued his lips to the left breast, and his teeth playfully bit and teased the nipple. Soon his hands moved like conquerors across her taut belly and sought the hem of her gown. He pulled it up so her loins were naked and open to him. Slowly, using his middle finger, he began moving it between her thighs and up and down across the length of her vaginal lips. There was none of the excitement she had felt the night at the beach... none of the beauty and none of the fire. Only numbness: a deadening absence of sensation. Jenny quivered in fright, and Bill took the motion to mean that she was shivering in excitement. "Like that," he asked, not waiting for an answer. He tweaked her clitoris. She felt nothing, could feel nothing. It was as though her body now was elsewhere. Her husband was fondling a wax statue.

Then Bill suddenly rose up in bed. She felt him struggling with his pyjamas. He removed his top... then kicked the bottoms out of bed where they lay in a heap on the floor. When he stretched out full-length beside her, she could feel the hair on his chest against her bare shoulder, his hairy legs against her smooth ones, and, and... that thing! Which seemed hotter and larger than ever.

She was absolutely cold with terror when Bill gently spread her legs apart. Then he swung his legs over her thigh and put his knee between her legs. A moment later he was hovering over her and kneeling between her legs. Jenny lay there, close to panic, trembling with a fear that Bill mistakenly accepted as desire.

She felt him fumbling for a moment, then the head of his hardened penis was pressing against the still dry lips of her vagina. When he touched her with it, it was as if someone had stuck a soldering iron against her bare unprotected skin.

"Don't hurt me, Bill... please. Oh, God... don't hurt me," she whimpered, trying to press herself into the mattress.

Bill was breathing heavily and he did not answer. He still reacted in a gentle fashion, however. He slowly pushed forward, spreading the curly pubic hair and the head of his cock slipped into the virginal portals of her vagina. She winced, "You're hurting me."

He moved the head of his prick in and out between the red full lips of her vagina; he did not seek to penetrate, merely to lubricate it. In spite of all her fear, Jenny could feel a moistness beginning down there as her body responded automatically. Perhaps, she thought, it will be all right, after all.

Then, he began to really hurt her when he attempted to push it in even further between her thighs. "No... Bill... Stop!" Bill stopped. And she repeated, "You're hurting me."

It was then he said it. She heard it and interpreted it as a confirmation of everything her mother had tried to warn her about. He said, "It always hurts a little the first couple of times."

"No, then. I don't want to do it!" she whimpered.

"Yes, you do," he insisted, and pressed his now heavily throbbing cock in a bit further.

"No... please." She felt as though he were already ripping her apart and he had only the head in – what would happen when he tried to insert the other seven inches?

Suddenly, Bill made one hard long thrusting motion. "Gaaaaghhh!" she screamed. His hips fell heavily between her widely spread thighs, and she was pinned like a helpless butterfly to the bed.

"No... God! No," she cried aloud. "Help me..." The words simply goaded Bill on to almost a maniacal frenzy. He shoved his pelvis hard into her

squirming defenceless crotch... seeking to reach that soft yielding belly that had been denied to him for over a year. She was squealing like a stuck pig as his cock reached the hymen and ripped through it like tissue paper touched with a glowing red poker. She splayed her legs out widely in the air in an effort to spread her cunt even wider – seeking to ease the agony... but it was hopeless. The cruel impalement was killing her, and he still did not have it all the way in. Down, down, down, ever deeper his rampaging cock ripped until she could feel the agonizing head of it finally coming to rest buried all the way to what seemed to be her navel. His rigid fleshy column was there only a second; he didn't even give her a chance to adjust to it. His motions – back and forth – became a wild demented thing. He pulled out, slammed it in – seemingly attempting to drive it ever deeper into her tortured pain-filled belly. Finally – and it seemed an eternity, although it couldn't have been more than a minute or two later, she felt his prick begin to throb as the hot eager cum spurted from him and flooded her virginal womb.

All in all, he came three more times before he finally pulled his penis from her vagina, before he stopped violating her body and went to sleep. Each time he had grunted and groaned out his climax and she had felt it spurting inside her, it was more painful, more disgusting than the first. Jenny wept silently. Her vagina was a throbbing nest of agony, and her silent desperate screams echoed through her mind and she saw her mother's tightly pressed lips saying, "See... I tried to tell you."

At dawn the phone rang. Jenny, who had not really slept, wearily reached over to the bedside table and answered. The hotel switchboard operator cheerfully sang, "Good morning. It's five-thirty."

"Thank you," Jenny said, without feeling.

Beside her, Bill stirred and groaned. "Whatimeizit?" he mumbled.

"Five-thirty," Jenny answered. "The airport limousine leaves at seven. I'll take my shower first, if you like."

Bill cocked one eye at her and made a sleepy effort to grin lewdly. "Why don't we both shower together?"

"No..." she shook her head. "No."

He shrugged. "Okay, you take yours first." He rolled over on his side and was asleep again before she could answer.

Jenny got out of bed, wincing at the painful tenderness in her abdomen. Her belly actually felt as if someone had repeatedly kicked her there. She felt as if she had been cut open in the crotch, as if a stripped corncob had been shoved in there. When she looked down at the sheet, she saw it was matted over a large area with brown blood and dried semen. Wide-eyed in horror, and with the room swirling around her, she gazed at her new peignoir. There was blood and sperm all over it – front, back, hemline and bodice. She ran for the bathroom, put her head into the toilet bowl, and vomited. When she took off her gown later, she had blood and semen all over her legs and in her pubic hair and on her stomach and buttocks. It looked as though she had been wallowing in a slaughterhouse trough.

She used almost an entire bar of soap cleaning herself, but it did no good. She still felt dirty... degraded.

When she got out of the shower and began towelling herself, she noticed that the blood had again begun to seep from her broken hymen.

CHAPTER FOUR

Bill wheeled the rental car around a curve on the side of a hill and saw the castle down below on the shores of a rather large, blue pear-shaped loch. The sight looked like something seen on a travel poster. He glanced over to see if Jenny had awakened yet, but she slept on. The poor kid, he thought; she had said she hadn't been able to sleep at all for the last three nights. He put it down to bridal nerves, just as he put down her coldness and reluctance to participate in the sex act to nerves. She had slept the sleep of the dead on the seven-hour flight over – not even waking for supper.

Gently, he reached out and shook her awake. "Jenny, we're here."

She came awake slowly, her mind swimming reluctantly to the surface of consciousness. Then she remembered and abruptly sat upright. Her muscles ached and her entire body felt as if she had been drugged. Bill was smiling at her, and suddenly she felt a great wave of tenderness and love go out to him. Now that she had had some rest, she was once more determined to make him a good wife. She loved him. That and the knowledge that he loved her would be enough for her. She would permit him sex – as much sex as he wanted – and she hoped and prayed that he would never know how much pain he was bringing her each time he invaded her body. When they returned home, she would quietly go to a doctor and get some suppositories to make her numb down there, something to deaden the nerves.

Impulsively, she bent over and kissed his cheek.

Bill nodded his head toward the window. "The castle," he said.

Jenny took a deep breath when she saw the loch. At the far end, a small sailboat was a dot of white against a blue and green canvas. Behind the castle, green hills rose steeply, and beyond them she could make out yet more hills fading to a delicate purple and mauve towards a distant horizon. On the other side a dense forest came down to the water's edge. It was a land for long hikes, of walking hand in hand, and communing with nature. Below her, the castle looked as if it had come out of some fairy tale; she saw that there was a small wooden jetty and a large white sandy beach.

"Oh, Bill, darling. It's so beautiful." This sight alone had made the journey worthwhile, she thought.

Bill grinned at Jenny's sparkling eyes and childlike enthusiasm. It was the first time since before the wedding that she had seemed her old self – happy, vivacious, and affectionate. Last night at the hotel, he had moments when he felt as if he were raping a stranger. He simply didn't understand it. Hell, after he had made love to her the fourth time, he had been able to sleep like a baby. Yet, apparently, she hadn't slept at all. And she hadn't come, either, even thought he had prolonged his lovemaking in an effort to get her there. When he thought about, she was the first woman – out of the dozens he had had – that he hadn't been able to build up to a rip-roaring climax. But, of course, she was his first virgin... and maybe virgins react differently, he supposed.

The car swept down the hill, across a small stone bridge, and reached the level. Two large Irish wolfhounds met them at the wrought-iron gate. The dogs, barking furiously, ran alongside the car until they reached the front of the castle.

At this distance, the noble edifice looked even larger than it had from afar. Because of the mass of turrets and towers, wasn't easy to determine the building's exact shape, but there was a tall, central block supported by two wings that formed three sides of a large, cobble-stoned, central courtyard that gave on to an outer courtyard, in turn accessed by a low, gated arch.

The dogs stopped barking and sat on their haunches, gazing expectantly at Bill and Jenny, staring at the couple almost as if asking, "Well, aren't you going to get out?"

Bill stepped out of the car and was scratching

one of the dogs behind the ear when he saw the woman coming toward them. Tall, full-breasted, black hair cut short, and wearing a long tartan dress that accentuated her splendid mature figure, she smiled and waved in greeting. In one arm, she carried a large bouquet of long stemmed red roses. A wide generous mouth, smouldering passionate black eyes with heavy black eyebrows, and the rich tan indicated more than a little Latin blood in her veins. Bill thought with some delight and an instinctive tightening in his groin: My God, what a sexy woman! And Jenny, with considerable envy, felt almost childlike opposite her.

"Hallo," she said warmly. "I'm Mary McAlister. You must be Bill and Jenny Grayson." Her voice was melodic and deep, with just a hint of Scottish in it.

"We are," Jenny answered, smiling timidly at her.

"These are for you, Jenny, from the garden. I picked them this morning," Mary said, holding out the roses. Then she held out her hand to Bill. "Hello... welcome to Castle Strathblane," she said again, shaking hands with him. Her grip was especially strong for a woman, and she had a disconcerting way of looking at a man... gazing right at him with such intensity that Bill felt as if he were drowning in her eyes. And, even though he was on his honeymoon, Bill knew with a sudden guilty feeling that he would like nothing better than to have those long legs wrapped around his buttocks, those breasts straining against his chest, and those

full lips tightened back against her teeth in lust...
as he pounded his hardened cock into her steaming
pussy.

Mary's lower lip dropped almost imperceptibly
as if she knew what be was thinking. Then she
turned to Jenny. "You must be exhausted after your
long journey. Come, I'll take you to your room so
you can freshen up." When Bill started to grab the
bags, she shook her head. "No... leave them," she
ordered. "I'll have one of the boys bring them up
to you."

Bill watched the two women walking in front of
him; it was not a good comparison. Mary obviously
was all woman – and very, very sure of herself. The
long dress covered her limbs, but if her legs were
like the rest of her – arms, breasts, hips – then
they would be perfect too. Jenny? Well, Jenny had
every bit as good a figure – not quite as tall, but
offsetting this was her undeniable femininity, a sort
of helplessness that made a male want to protect
her. Actually, aside from colouring and height, the
main difference between the two women lay in
their projected sensuality and poise. Jenny seemed
almost adolescently self-conscious as she walked
next to Mary, and if Bill had been able to read
Jenny's mind at that very moment he would have
realized just how inferior his wife felt.

Mary led them to a spacious, beautifully
decorated room on the third floor. Large picture
windows looked out over the loch and distant hills.
"This is your sitting room," Mary said. "Wood for
the fireplace is in the box there, though I doubt

you'll be needing a fire in this glorious weather." She opened a connecting door. "This is your bedroom. I'm sure you'll find it comfortable." There was a big king-sized bed under a blue and white striped canopy. She indicated another door, "And the shower..." The shower, Bill noted, was large enough for three people; it had an overhead nozzle and two fine spray nozzles which shot a stream of water midriff – front and back. Bill couldn't help thinking, "What a great play pen." Something must have shown on his face, because Mary's eyes twinkled and Jenny blushed.

"My husband and I would like you to be our guests for cocktails before joining us at dinner this evening," Mary said.

Jenny glanced at Bill, who replied, "That's very kind of you, Mrs. McAlister."

"You must call me Mary. And Dr. McAlister will certainly insist that you call him John."

"All right, Mary," Bill said. "What time?"

"Well... let's see. You're the only guests we have at the moment. The castle's other owner, Lord Drymuir and his sister, Lady Liza Huntly, will be arriving tomorrow; then we have another young American couple checking in on Thursday. So we can be flexible about dinner time tonight. An hour from now?"

Jenny felt grimy after the flight and car trip. She said, "I would like to take a shower, and change into something else."

Mary was immediately apologetic. "Of course, my dear. How thoughtless of me. I'll have your bags brought up at once." She glanced at her watch. "It's five thirty now. Shall we say seven-thirty-ish?"

Neither Jenny nor Bill were prepared for Dr. McAlister when they met him two hours later. He had a stern military bearing about him, which was deceptive, for he turned out to be just as warm and friendly as Mary. And, as his wife had said, he did insist on being called 'John'. He was at least two inches taller than Bill's six feet, and weighed in the neighborhood of 220 pounds – and it was a lean 220 pounds at that. A grey moustache cut a thin line across his lips. All in all, Jenny thought as she stared at him in open admiration, he cuts a dashing figure... like something out of a Scotch whisky ad or a suspense film about Scotland Yard. He, like his wife, exuded an almost animalistic sensuality. Side by side, the McAlister couple definitely would be attention-getters, even in a crowd of sophisticates.

Bill and Jenny both felt at ease with them during cocktails in the huge library. This was surprising in view of the fact that Mary was in her mid thirties and John probably in his middle or late forties.

From the library, they went to the baronial hall-like dining room where a dour and silent old serving maid served the four of them. It was not until the final course that Jenny got around to asking, "What kind of a doctor are you, John?"

"A retired one," he said, smiling mysteriously as he held up his wine glass to the candlelight and inspected its contents.

Mary said, "John! Don't tease." She turned to Jenny and said, "He was a gynaecologist – a very successful and famous one, I might add."

John snorted as though enjoying a private joke and his wife flashed a look of warning. As brief as it was, it sufficed, for the man came back to his winning ways again. "All sorts of rich ladies with all sorts of rich ladies' problems." He shrugged and laughed. "A very lucrative profession. I made enough in ten years to buy a half-share in Strathblane from my cousin, Lord Drymuir. Together we set out to refurbish a much-neglected, lovely old building – a sort of joint project, if you like.

Mary commented, "Actually John is much too modest. He has a great many other talents. Right now he's doing some very important research on ESP."

"ESP?" Jenny asked.

"Extra sensory perception," Mary explained.

John, who was rolling a fork back and forth between his thumb and forefinger, looked up and said, "It's mainly a hobby – something to keep me busy – although the government is interested in the experiments. I believe that ESP can be enhanced by putting a person in a light hypnotic state; then we place someone very close to this person in another room and attempt to establish communication between the two."

Bill, whose eyes had widened, said unbelievingly, "You mean mental telepathy?"

John nodded, and smiled. "I can understand your doubt. I'd be incredulous myself if I hadn't received proof that it seems to work... at least with some people."

Jenny was sitting there engrossed, in rapt attention. This was the most fascinating thing she had ever listened to in her life.

Mary said casually, "Why not try the basic experiment tonight, using Bill and Jenny? Let them see for themselves."

"Oh, could we?" Jenny blurted out.

Bill added quickly, "That would be one sure way of making a believer out of me."

McAlister shook his head and frowned. "No... I don't think it's..."

Jenny interrupted, pleading in a little girl's voice, "Please?"

Mary laughed, "You've piqued their curiosity, John. You won't be a good host unless you show them how it works."

McAlister glanced from Bill to Jenny and then over to Mary. He pursed his lips and said, with considerable reluctance in his voice, "I generally need more time to get to know my subjects better." He looked thoughtful, then nodded, "All right. Let's try it anyway. It may not work, but..." he held out his hands, palms up, and smiled, "we'll see."

Jenny was feeling slightly apprehensive when she followed the McAlisters into the library. She had never been hypnotized before; it would be a novel experience... and a little frightening. Bill, now that he had shot off his mouth, was suffering some qualms also.

McAlister moved a large dark green leather chair

out into the centre of the room and then turned a rheostat in the wall until the lights dimmed. A switch was pushed and a thin beam shone down from a spotlight on the beamed ceiling. "Jenny, you sit here." Soft harp and flute music floated out of hidden stereo speakers.

Shivering with suppressed excitement, Jenny did as she was told. With considerable ceremony, McAlister took down a black leather box from the mantel. He opened it and brought out into the light a green pear-shaped amulet on a gold chain. Then he removed a sealed white envelope and handed it to Bill. "These are your test messages. So you won't think it's some kind of a trick, I would like Jenny to give you three numbers between one and twenty before you leave this room. You will read and follow the directions opposite each of the numbers. For example, if she said 'four, eighteen and twenty', you would read paragraph four – where it says you are to concentrate on an image of a tiger in the jungle. Paragraphs eighteen and twenty are, of course, on different subjects. Understand?"

Bill nodded. Mary took his arm and said, "Come on. Our station is in the waiting room across the hall." Bill was all too aware of her hand on his arm; her presence up close was a tangible thing, and the musky scent of her perfume was as elusive as a night bird's call.

"Wait!" McAlister ordered. "You don't have your numbers." He turned to the girl, "All right, Jenny."

She pursed her lips in thought, then blinked and

smiled. "Three, seven and... ah... fourteen."

As Mary lead him out of the room, Bill found his eyes fastened on the pendant dangling from McAlister's hand. He would like to have remained and see Jenny go under, but obviously that was not part of the experiment.

When they got to the waiting room, Mary reached in front of him to open the massive door. The bodice of her crepe dinner gown gaped open and Bill saw – with an immediate feeling of hunger – that she was not wearing a bra for those magnificent breasts. Quickly, he forced his eyes away. He thought Mary looked amused. "Sit here," she said, motioning to the couch. He sat, as ordered. Mary seated herself beside him and handed over the envelope to be opened. "Three, seven and fourteen," she said.

Bill ripped the envelope open and withdrew several typewritten sheets of paper.

"Do you mind if I read over your shoulder?" Mary asked, and the perfume of her breath was almost an aphrodisiac of its own. She didn't wait for permission, but slid right over until their bodies were touching. The heat of her thigh was like a blow torch there. Bill swallowed; he could feel desire for this woman beginning to boil up in him. He wondered, for about the twentieth time since their first meeting, how she would be in bed... how it would feel to have his hardened cock buried deep inside those glorious loins. Mary leaned forward in order to see the paper better, and once again her gown gaped. Seemingly without thinking, she put her hand on his knee. Her lips were only inches away as she began to read aloud, "Number three: you are to think of a train. The cars will flash past you and you will concentrate on the windows and the faces of people inside the car. A close relative of the subject being communicated with should be one of the faces you concentrate on... a mother, father, sister, but not yourself." Mary remained in close after she had finished reading; Bill could feel her left breast against his upper arm. "Christ," he said to himself, "how can I concentrate with those tits. Mary had better watch it or I'm going to make a grab for her... that'll really fuck up the honeymoon."

His voice was hoarse and uncertain when he asked, "How long does it take to hypnotize her?"

Mary drew back just a bit. "Only seconds if she's susceptible. Many people can't be hypnotized, however. In that case, John will probably want to hypnotize you instead of Jenny."

In the library, McAlister was just completing his incantation as he swung the glowing amulet in front of the girl's glazed and unseeing eyes. "You are so drowsy... so sleepy... you cannot keep your eyes open. Sleep... sleep... sleep." Jenny's head fell to her chest. McAlister dropped the pendant back into the box and then withdrew a needle, which he pricked against the girl's shapely right buttock. She did not stir. Satisfied, he said, "Jenny... can you hear me?"

"Yes..."

"Jenny... at two o'clock tomorrow morning, you

will awaken to find your husband getting into bed with you. It may look like me... but it will be your husband. Do you understand?"

"It will be my husband."

"Yes, it will be your husband. Now, when I count to ten, you will begin to wake up. You will not remember being hypnotized; hypnosis did not work with you. You will recall nothing. One, two, three... seven, eight..." He snapped his fingers, and Jenny's eyes blinked open.

Jenny had felt that she couldn't be hypnotized, now as she sat in the chair waiting for Dr. McAlister to try, she was positive it would not work. McAlister pulled up a stool in front of her; he held up the pendant and began swaying it to and fro in front of her eyes. "You are getting sleepy," he said.

Jenny giggled. It was an involuntary thing, quickly suppressed. McAlister gave her a mock frown. "You must be serious about this, young lady, or I won't be able to hypnotize you."

She was immediately contrite. "I'm sorry, John. It's just that I don't think I'm going to be a good subject."

"Well, we'll see," McAlister said professionally, and went back to his incantations. Jenny listened to him, she attempted to concentrate on what he said, but she didn't get sleepy at all. Finally, even John admitted that she was a difficult subject. He stood and sighed in dejection, "Maybe we should try Bill. If I can put him under, you can serve as the communicator."

Bill was reluctant to be a guinea pig; however,

when he saw the disappointment on Jenny's face and the mocking expression on Mary's, he decided to go along with the gag. "I won't fight you," he told John, "but I don't really think you can do it."

McAlister merely shrugged. "It's possible I can't. Your wife wasn't susceptible to hypnosis." He laughed. "I almost put myself to sleep."

McAlister adjusted the spotlight beam for Bill's added height and withdrew the pendant again, "Now watch the jewel as it swings... back and forth... back... and forth... in front of you. Keep your eyes on it, Bill... concentrate on it as it swings... back and forth... See how the light seems to glow from deep within..."

Two minutes later, McAlister stood with an evil smirk on his face. "You silly young ass. Can't hypnotize you... eh?" He jabbed the needle into Bill's calf; the boy did not move. "All right, Bill. At two o'clock tomorrow morning, you will get out of bed and walk down the hallway to the end, turn left and walk to the end of that hallway, then you are to go through the open door on the right. You will get into bed with your wife; you will want to please her in whatever way you can. You will do exactly what she asks – everything she asks. It will be your wife... although it may look like Mary... it will be your wife. Do you understand?"

"I will do anything my wife wants... it will be my wife."

"Yes, it will be your wife. Now when I count to ten, you will begin to wake up. You will not remember being hypnotized; hypnosis did not work with you. One, two, three..."

Bill was having a difficult time keeping a straight face as he waited for McAlister to try to hypnotize him. He was sure it wouldn't work, and he felt amusement – even pity – as McAlister picked up that cheap pendant and began swaying it in front of his eyes. Really, he thought, it was just like something from the movies during the early thirties. "Boy," he said to himself, "how cornball can you get?"

Half an hour later, after the final brandy of the evening, Bill and Jenny were still feeling somewhat guilty about the fact that McAlister had been unable to hypnotize either one of them. Both secretively felt, however, that it was because they had such strong will power.

"Goodnight... goodnight, thank you for a lovely evening... it was a pleasure... goodnight..."

Bill and Jenny climbed the three flights to their room. When Bill kissed her and pulled her toward the big couch in front of the fireplace, Jenny suddenly felt the earlier gaiety and happiness of the evening evaporate. It was, she thought, time for sex. Oh, how she hated that word... disgusting, degrading... pain-filled and terrible. She would have to let him do it to her once, and when or if he tried to do it twice, she would tell him that she was much too sore. He would understand, she thought.

Downstairs, a lewdly grinning John and Mary McAlister held up brandy snifters in a toast. "Here's to a good double fuck," McAlister said.

The catlike glow in Mary's eyes abruptly became

an all-consuming flame. "To a very good fuck," she said, "for us both!" She laughed shrilly. "I can hardly wait." And she repeated a statement she had made earlier to him. "My God! Did you see the size of his cock when he stepped out of the shower! Mammoth. Beautiful!" She gritted her teeth as she visualized once again the two of them looking through the bathroom's one-way mirror at the boy as he unsuspectingly towelled himself dry.

"I thought the girl had the finest little ass I've seen in years," McAlister said thoughtfully.

"Yes, you old bugger, you," Mary said cattily, digging her elbow into his ribs, "you would notice that! Well, everyone to their own tastes."

"You are being a bit of a bitch," John said, but it was said with affection.

Mary laughed gaily. "To a helluva good fuck," she said again, downing the rest of the brandy.

CHAPTER FIVE

Jenny abruptly came awake; it was as though a switch had been thrown in her body. She was fully aware of everything... the moonlight streaming in through the windows, the fading echoes of the clock downstairs striking two, the breathing of the man who stood beside the bed.

Perhaps it was the moonlight that made everything seem as though it were happening in a dream, that her mind was elsewhere – confined to limbo.

"Jenny?" Even Bill's voice seemed different, accented.

She turned and looked up at him. In the unreal light he seemed taller, older than Bill. He looked like someone she knew... but the vaporous quality of the moment refused to solidify. "This man is your husband," a voice in her brain whispered.

"Yes... Bill."

"Good, you're awake." The covers were pulled back and the figure slid into bed with her. She felt his body move in next to hers; then that body was pressing nakedly and urgently against her side. With a sudden tightening of her muscles and a feeling of despair, Jenny realized Bill had an erection and was probably going to try to make love to her again. Against her hip, his penis felt different – considerably smaller, but hard!

"Are you all right?" she asked, knowing full well what he wanted.

Bill laughed; he sounded so very different, but her mind kept saying, "This is your husband."

His voice said, "Well, darling. I'm not really all right. I have this problem which only you can take care of." He moved his penis suggestively up and down against her side.

"Bill, I don't think I can do it again tonight. I'm much too sore. It's so painful."

"Then we shall simply have to do it another way, won't we, pet?" He had taken her chin in his hand and turned her face toward him. His breath had a vaguely exciting hot brandy smell as his lips kissed her eyes closed. His hot wet tongue sought out her ear; she stiffened as it shot into the cavity like a small darting fish seeking shelter. The sensation, though strange, was definitely erotic. Bill had never kissed her this way before! Then his tongue was in her mouth, tracing wild abandoned designs against her teeth and inner folds of her lips. This, too, was exciting in a way it had never been before. She began responding eagerly; once, when her tongue hit his upper lip, she thought: How strange... Bill has grown a mustache.

"You wonderful creature," he said, just as his hands began moving all over her body. He went first to the flushed bulbs of her breasts, and each individual pore of his fingers seemed to be minute vacuums tugging at her flesh. He tongue-kissed her again, then his lips fastened – gently sucking – at a place where her gracefully sloping neck muscles joined the top of the shoulder. A tingle of excitement arched along the muscles. He moved her elbow out from the body and his mouth moved down until it was licking and kissing the sensitive flesh on the inner arm and armpit. A moment later, slowly and tantalizingly, his lips kissed their way to the left breast. She felt him there at her nipple, like a thirsty person sucking juice from luscious fruit. Not once, in his gentleness, did he hurt her.

As his teeth teased sensuously at her nipples and his knowing hands kneaded the flesh of her buttocks, Jenny suddenly realized that her body was reacting... in a most pleasurable manner. She purred deep in her throat as his lips moved on to her right breast, then to her right armpit, and traced an exciting trail of fiery desire down across her rib cage to her navel. One of his hands left the pleasantly tingling mounds of flesh on her buttocks and, using the fingertips only, began stroking the underside of her knee and the soft inner sides of her thigh.

"Ummmm," she purred, as his tongue flickered at her navel. Jenny wasn't exactly sure when his fingertips brushed against her pubic hair, all she knew for sure was that suddenly he had reached the vagina. She gave a little gasp of fright and flattened her buttocks down into the mattress; his hand was trapped, unable to move. He sought to move his fingers, but her thighs were like a hot flesh vise.

"Jenny," he said, "open your legs."

"No... it hurts."

"Daddy will kiss it to make it better."

What had he said? What did he mean? Kiss it? "Bill?" she began questioningly, but she had her answer in the next moment, for his tongue had left the warm little cave of her belly button and marched boldly across the bare plains of her abdomen and into the silken forest of her luxuriant pubic hair.

"Bill?" she groaned again, not certain exactly what he was doing. In her anxiety, or perhaps it was merely subconscious desire, she eased the pressure of her thighs and his hand was freed from captivity. She tensed again as he nuzzled his cheek in the fleece of her pubic mound and used his thumb and forefinger to slightly separate the soft fleshy lips of her vagina. Oddly enough, he was so gentle that she hardly felt his touch, much less pain. She was suffering from apprehension and indecision, however. Whatever Bill had in mind was something totally alien to her – something she had never heard about, never even suspected. He moved his head down to her thigh and kissed it – starting once again with that extremely sensitive area behind the knee, moving upward – ever upward – occasionally taking large sucking erotic bites of the inner thigh flesh into his mouth, and at other times using his tongue as a stylus to sear flaming trails of desire into her trembling body.

Then his tongue reached the soft protruding folds of her young pulsating pussy. She sat upright, forcing his head away. "No, Bill. No."

"Why not?"

"I hurt there."

"I'll kiss it to make it better," he repeated softly, his voice droning smoothly like a recording.

"No... it still hurts." She pulled his head up to breast level. She felt it necessary to say something – anything! She took a deep breath. "Bill, I've never told you this. I don't know why I'm saying it now. But you must be gentle and understanding with me. My mother and her mother and all the females on my mother's side for as far back as we can remember have had something wrong with them. I didn't know about it until the day before the marriage or I would have told you. Sexual intercourse is extremely painful... it hurts. So you must be gentle and not expect too much out of me."

Even as she said it, her mind was reeling in guilt and she felt like weeping. She had planned to keep this her secret; and now, for some reason, she was blurting it out. Maybe, she thought desperately, I'm really looking for help... maybe Bill and I working can solve this thing. She was not prepared for his sudden bark of laughter.

"What absolute rubbish," he said, unkindly.

"I mean it, Bill," she said, pleading for understanding.

"Look, my little pet, I know something – a great deal – about women's problems. What you claim is something that simply is not organically possible. Psychologically possible, yes! We have a name for acute painful sexual intercourse. It's called mental vaginismus, or more plainly, monosymptomatic hysteria. Get that word 'hysteria', because that's exactly what it is – a form of nervous hysteria."

"I tell you it hurts; it's excruciating."

"You think it hurts. You've been brain-washed. And I am going to prove it. Remember, I am your... husband. Repeat that!"

"You think it hurts. You've been brainwashed." She heard the words, they seemed to come from someone other than herself. She had no will to resist; her body felt as though it had turned to foam rubber.

"I am your husband and I will not harm you... You will answer my questions truthfully."

"I will answer... your questions truth...fully."

"Jenny, have you ever reached a climax – had an orgasm? Any kind of orgasm, even from masturbation?"

"No... I have never masturbated to... completion. It is self-abuse... sinful."

"I thought so. All right, now lie there... relax... and let your body speak to you about how it really feels." He began kissing her breasts again.

His mouth moved away from her breasts after a moment and began nibbling at the small fold of flesh right below her navel. He gently bit a particularly sensitive area where her hip bone and upper thighs joined. Her body had begun to purr again. Then his hot hungry mouth spread the soft fleecy pubic hair and fastened over the fleshy opening of the vaginal tunnel leading to her womb. A sudden jolt of pure feeling arched through her loins as he began noisily sucking the vaginal lips; it was a gentle vacuum, tugging and caressing the nerve ends. "Aahhhh," she crooned softly.

"Ahhhh!" she repeated, this time loudly, as his tongue began licking the entire length of her open cuntal slit – running from anus to clitoris.

"Ahhh... oooooh," she gasped, as first his lips and then his teeth found the hard little clitoris. She strained her hips up to his mouth, arching her back and planting her feet in the mattress in an effort to rise and meet him.

"AAHHH... AHEEEEE!" she screamed, as his hot quivering tongue went boldly into the tunnel of her cunt, moving in and out as though it were a small sure penis. She was aware that her breath was coming raggedly from her taut lips, that she had reached down to his head – not to push him away, but to keep him there... forever! Some shrill hysterical voice – which sounded somewhat like a tinny hollow echo of Mother's – was screaming in the nethermost regions of her mind that this was wicked, perverted, that it was painful! The gratifying, wonderful sensations in her snatch pushed that shrill voice back, back, back until it was obliterated by another scream; this scream was one of passion boiling out of her lips, out of her soul.

Oh, how his tongue and lips and teeth all worked together in a fully orchestrated symphony of pure feeling! She could feel things happening down there – wild, uninhibited, beautiful things... of nerve endings singing and screaming in delight, of muscles flexing and unflexing in joy, of flesh and bone and pores all in harmony. She was revolving her hips in a grinding, circular motion against his avaricious, indomitable mouth.

"Don't stop, Bill. Oh, God... don't stop, darling!" she panted, for now something else was happening down there. Everything was rubbing against each other – like nylon and wool – throwing off sparks which were igniting the ganglions. She had never thought she would feel this; she thought she was incapable of it. And then, as though a miracle, she was coming! She could tell because body and soul were separating.

"Uh... uhhh? Ahhh... ah... ah... ah?" It was a question, a plea! She raised her buttocks clear up from the mattress and, as she did so, his tongue left her vagina and his teeth and lips clamped hard on her gently pulsating clitoris. She screamed, and she knew she was screaming loudly. "Go on... Go on. Go!" Now, like desert mirages in midday's heat, her womb began to dissolve – shimmering into incandescent nothingness. Her insides had become roaring cataracts racing and dancing toward the sea... and their white waters bubbled, raged, boiled, and spurted from her cunt – like torrents from a broken dam – as she screamed again, "I'm coming!" There was nothing in the universe but that one great pit and pendulum of sensation and release. Her ears heard not, her eyes saw not, her mind thought not. Only the cunt was there – the almighty cunt! – stronger than all her other organs put together, and it screamed out a song of ecstasy that would not be denied. That sweet, intolerable delight stayed with her for ten million eternities, and during it all she lay gasping, and thrashing that only sentiment thing in her body against his voraciously hungry lips.

It finally ended. Not with a bang, but like the slow fading of Summer's first sunset. She felt him kiss the warm flooded area between her thighs once more then his mouth moved back to her hips. She could feel her cum cool and damp on her thighs and buttocks. Then he used his free hand to turn her on her side. He kissed the right buttock, then continued to press her over until she was lying face down. Jenny didn't resist; her will power had been completely vapourized by the velvet explosion that had only moments ago torn her still quivering belly asunder.

Sensation was slow to return, but when it did, she was aware that he was reverently kissing her smooth, oval buttocks. Occasionally, he would desist to lick a teasingly sensitive spot at the base of her spine, but he always came back to the soft rounded mounds of flesh to kiss and gently nibble. A warm glow began to spread throughout her anal area as new and recharged blood pounded through the revitalized muscle paths, arteries and capillaries.

She heard him mutter as though he were an art connoisseur, "Such untouched beauty... such a sweet, young little arse... so supple, so soft and warm, so charmingly shaped and virginal."

Now he gradually began to change his activity there. He interspersed his kisses with occasional sharp little bites. They weren't painful – not too painful. They were, she had to admit, rather exciting. Jenny sensed he was getting ready to do something different again, and she mentally told herself that no matter what he did it would be heavenly if it were even only half as delightful as the thing he had just done. Nothing, though, bad prepared her for what came next. His kisses, his rabbitlike nibbling, became more urgent. Suddenly, he pushed her legs apart and then knelt behind her. She felt him use his thumbs to spread her soft yielding buttocks wide apart and then... his tongue was moving again, now licking the inner crevice that joined her vaginal slit below.

Once she had recovered from her momentary flush of embarrassment, she thought that it was an odd sensation. Not displeasing, not really

pleasurable or erotic... "strange" was the word. His hot, wet, trembling tongue moved the length of her anal crevice; she felt the first stirrings of excitement when it lingered over the base of her spine again. Then he backed off and down. "Bill," she gasped, as she felt his tongue tip quiver against and then wetly worm its way into her tiny puckered anus. A forbidden, wicked pleasure shot through her loins. "You mustn't," she groaned, "it's not right."

Now he pulled his mouth away. "Anything is right between a man and a woman – so long as it gives pleasure and not offence. And I know you're having pleasure... you're a natural for this. Believe me, I can tell."

"But... but..."

He laughed. "'But' is right. You have a delightful little 'butt'. And I'm going to make love to you there. I'm going to fuck you there, Jenny."

"Oh no, darling, you can't," she protested.

"And pray tell, why not?"

"It isn't right, darling it just isn't right," she moaned down into the pillow.

He repeated, "Anything is right between a husband and wife," Then he lowered his head again. She felt his hands beneath her hips pulling her belly up off the mattress. She wasn't kneeling exactly, but her smooth rounded buttocks waved up in the air like an ostrich's. She felt foolish in that position; she felt obscenely naked with her unprotected behind upturned that way. But, still, he was her husband... and he wouldn't hurt her?

She felt his tongue leave her anus, to be replaced

by a finger that probed as if it, too, wanted to enter the tight forbidden passageway and she immediately tensed. Then suddenly, he reached up, grabbed a pillow, and slipped it beneath her stomach to keep her from falling flat again. At the same time, the finger back there had begun a gentle little sawing movement against her delectably puckered anal ring. Now he was pressing in harder, while Jenny clenched her anal ring tighter and tighter. She winced and groaned, trying to push her belly down into a pillow and abruptly the fingernail portion of the digit was inside her. She was rather surprised. Somehow she had thought it would hurt, but it didn't. It was, if she were honest with herself, sort of pleasant... as long as she relaxed and didn't fight it.

Now he was sawing continuously – nothing abrupt – always gentle, but always pressing in a bit deeper. She moved her hips experimentally, then discovered the best movement was one using the leg and belly muscles to raise her buttocks back.

"That's a good girl," he said soothingly. "Such a good girl, with such a fine little arsehole. You'll need next to no instruction. Pure instinct, I wager."

"Bill, you mustn't talk like that," she protested through her soft mewls of pleasure. Her protest was rewarded by laughter from him.

Finally the finger was in all the way up to the knuckle and his palm was pressing tightly against the cheeks of her buttocks as he began to make tiny circular motions inside with his finger – almost as if he wanted to expand the opening. A moment later, the first finger withdrew. She wanted to pass wind, but held back – much too embarrassed. When the finger returned, it seemed much thicker. Then she realized he was using two fingers. "That hurts," she whimpered slightly, knowing it was a lie but feeling she had to protest anyway.

"Be calm, my love. It can't hurt very much... you'll be fine in a second."

Actually, she thought, it really wasn't painful... but she knew she was being stretched there. She supposed that his two fingers, however, were less in diameter than her evacuations; she remembered as a child having wondered how something so large could come from such a tiny opening.

The two fingers were sawing in concert now. She wiggled her buttocks in the air and she felt her muscles, deep in her belly, milk at the finger. This brought delighted laughter from her husband.

"Wait," he said, "until I get in there... then do it all you want." He took a deep breath, "I knew you were a natural."

Jenny's thoughts were jumbled. She knew instinctively that this wasn't right. Yet, at the same time, it was mysteriously exciting. She felt subjugated, completely at the mercy of her husband. She blushed deeply when the pressures became so intense that she farted loudly. The sound was rewarded by a laugh and a hard bite on her right buttocks. His two fingers made circular motions in her rectum; it was being stretched... stretched... stretched. Now she began to feel a compelling urge to have his fingers in there deeper. She pushed back against them, groaning slightly once as she felt his fingernail hang up against a fold of membrane, and tossed her head in wild abandon from side to side in rhythm with his finger fucking motions in her rectum.

Then suddenly he withdrew his fingers. She could feel the rubbery elastic ring of her asshole clinging to them – reluctant to let them go. And then, out they came with a wet hissing noise like that of a deflating balloon.

She turned her head, disappointed, to find out why he had stopped. He was stroking his penis, and she could see the thick white foreskin moving back and forth over the instrument's head. Then he was between her legs. His hands reached beneath her and cupped her thighs – holding them tightly. She felt him move forward until his penis was pressing against the puckered brown aperture. She suddenly realized that his prick was considerably larger than just two fingers; she wouldn't be able to take it. He should be able to see that! Still, the pressure continued, the prick moving gently, always gently, gradually insinuating its way through the tiny tight opening stretching it wider and wider until finally the head of it was completely in. She was pleasantly surprised, even proud of herself; it hadn't hurt very much at all.

"Try to shit or fart," her husband said.

"Bill!" It was a shock to hear him use language like that.

"Try... it'll go in easier."

Jenny pressed down with her abdominal muscles

·and was relieved to discover that part of the pressure had been removed. It was fine... just fine.

She felt him begin to move in deeper, and all of a sudden – at about the two inch mark – he began to hurt her, terribly. She tried to push forward into the pillow, but his hands held her thighs captive.

"That hurts," she winced, meaning it this time. "It's hurting horribly!"

He paid no attention to her... just continued his inexorable pressure inward.

Now there was genuine pain in the pit of her stomach. Not vaginal pain, but pain from her protesting bowels as the fleshy reaming rod moved deeper and deeper against the normal flow of traffic in the rectum. "It's too big," she whimpered. "Please stop! Oh God, darling, please stop!"

Escape was impossible. She was impaled there like a captured blonde butterfly. He was using her body like a wheelbarrow, his hands holding her thighs, his legs keeping her legs well separated.

"Raise up," he ordered.

It was so painful that she would gladly obey any order, just to relieve the pain. She raised her buttocks a bit, and the prick slid smoothly and deeper into her rectum. It moved quickly until suddenly she felt his pubic hair slap hard against her ass.

"Gaaaggh," she groaned. God, how it hurts! It was simply impossible to think. The pain was even more intense because now she was feeling degraded, abused. The excitement she had felt with his fingers in there had gone – being ripped away by the reality and overpowering presence of that hot, pulsating log lodged in her rectum.

He began moving in and out like a well-oiled piston. Her asshole made gasping, sucking noises with each movement. "Oh... hhh," she gasped with each new thrust inward.

He stopped for a moment, and Jenny realized he was panting in delight. He asked, "Do you remember what you did a moment ago with your belly muscles? I want you to do it again."

"I don't... know... what you... mean," she gasped through pain contorted lips, not really remembering.

"Imagine you are standing with your legs spread wide apart. Imagine you have a string attached to your navel; at the end of that string is an apple. Without moving your feet, lift the string. Lift your navel and pull the apple off the ground."

Jenny concentrated for a moment, then inhaled deeply and at the same time tightened and lifted her stomach muscles.

"Ahhhh... God!" he shouted, his voice gurgling with glee. "Again. Ahhhhh... Oh, God! Again... and again! Keep doing it, girl."

Each time she lifted the imaginary apple, she was rewarded with a joyous shout and a deeper thrust into her clenching anal passage. He sawed in and out of her asshole – rhythmically – plunging deep into those softer, darker areas of her being which she had never known existed.

Jenny had begun to feel a change in her rectum, and this was accomplished by a change in her attitude. She wanted to please her husband. She still felt degraded and helpless, but the mere hopelessness of her position made it all acceptable. She was beginning to experience some masochistic enjoyment from those thrusts, and she knew instinctively that she could enjoy them even more by rearing back to meet his thrusts. She began doing so, and was pleased by his low pitched moan of responding pleasure.

She moved her firm white buttocks in tiny little circles – weaving it in the air like a balloon on the end of its tether. She pulled up imaginary apples by the dozens; she pressed down as though she hadn't shit in a year. His yelps of contagious enjoyment encouraged her. Gradually, she began feeling a weird glow illuminating her inner bowels. It wasn't possible, she thought. Not this way... not this way! Can woman reach a climax this way too? Nerve ends were beginning to telegraph messages, and muscles were beginning to vibrate like steel rails predicting the imminent arrival of a train.

After a moment's experimentation, she discovered her rectal passage could be tightened two or three times at the apogee of each outward stroke – bringing greater pleasure to her and deeper groans of happiness from him. With the perigee of his inward thrust, she flexed her deepest anal muscle against the head of his cock. "God!" was all he said. She suddenly realized, as she tossed her head wantonly from side to side that she was enjoying this cruel debasement. She also realized, with a rapid catch of breath, that she could come like this if she worked at it... concentrated on it.

Now, breathing stentoriously, her husband pulled the hot throbbing cock all the way out to the glans, then shoved it desperately in as a prelude to the final act and curtain.

"Ahhhh," she moaned, and there was no longer any pain in her voice, only encouragement and lust.

Now, with long hard unending thrusts, he began to batter her quivering buttocks. He gasped like a man who had run the thousand-metre race. She was being skewered like a wounded carcass, split right down the middle. And she didn't care. She didn't care! She became aware of a velvet feeling throughout the pit of her stomach. Once again she thought: Could it be? Could it really be?

"Eeee... aaahhh..." He was making noises like a rusty door creaking open.

"Ahhh... ahhhh," she returned, attempting to say, "deeper, deeper, harder, harder," but unable to put the words into speech. She was astonished, hopeful... pleased.

Her head was tossing back and forth uncontrollably now as the two bodies moved like suddenly insane puppets released from their master's strings.

He murmured incoherently as his hands finally let go of her thighs, and she felt his fingernails cruelly bite into the folds of skin in front of her hipbones as he sought new purchase. It hurt her. It hurt her! And she wanted to be hurt!

Then she felt the one last mighty thrust which drove the swollen rod up to the furthest point it had been; she made her muscles up there grab hold of it and milk it. The prick spurted, then began twitching as he came deep, deep in the rectum, giving her a love enema. He cried out, and his strangled voice was the thing that triggered her own explosion... it was a different feeling than before... much different, deeper, a different set of muscles, nerves, and bones crying out their happy defiance to normality. "Ahhh... aieeeee!" she screamed, and above her own shouts, she could hear his, "Beautiful... wonderful... aaaahhhh." He smartly whacked at her blushing buttocks with his open hand as though he were encouraging a race horse on to greater effort.

Some time later, as she lay there feeling the velvet and warm satin of her glands and nerves, she seemed to hear the far-off sound of a stranger's voice saying, "You have been dreaming... dreaming. You will awaken tomorrow; it will have been a dream... about your husband. Tomorrow night, you will awaken at the same time and your husband will be your husband. Tonight was only a dream. Repeat please."

Her voice, from beyond the furthermost part of the galaxy, answered, "It was a dream. Tomorrow night I will awaken..."

And once, just before oblivion came to her, she thought she heard the satanic snicker of a triumphant male voice and a pair of hot lips reverently kissing her buttocks.

But, of course, it was all part of the dream... it had to be a dream... and deep in her mind and heart, she knew and felt disappointment that it had been just a dream...

CHAPTER SIX

Bill came slowly awake with the sound of dogs barking outside. He cocked one eye and stared up at the ceiling where a filigree of shadows was cast by the sun streaming through the ivy outside the window. He took a deep breath, slowly brought his hand out from beneath the covers, and stared at his watch. Nine o'clock. His prodigious yawn was cut short as he suddenly recalled the dream... about their hosts' wife!

He blinked. Yes, of course, it was a dream. He turned on his side and stared speculatively at the still sleeping Jenny. In his dream Mary had been his wife... no, that wasn't right either. It had been Jenny be made love to in his dream, only Jenny looked like Mary? Was that it?

He smiled secretively. No matter. It was one helluva wet dream. Boy, he'd had women go wild under him before, but nothing like Mary in the dream. She'd fought him like a marlin trying to shake a hook; the hook had been his prick, and he'd let her run, then reeled in, let her run again, and then finally brought her to gaff – panting and gasping. A real prize trophy. Tremendous. Unbelievably tremendous!

The dream had come tenuously. He remembered waking up next to Jenny... only it really wasn't

Jenny, it was Mary. Oh, to hell with it, he thought; what does it matter. The dream was the thing! In the dream he had awakened to find himself stripped and lying next to his nude wife. It was the way he had been awakened that was interesting. His wife had been fondly stroking his cock, crooning over it, admiring its size and beauty.

She had kissed him, and her mouth was all honey and heat and tongue. And she had placed his head against her breast and fed him like a hungry infant. And then she had stroked his cock again and told him she wanted it deep inside her.

His wife had said, "With a cock like yours, I want a real bread and butter fuck, at least the first time. Tomorrow night, you're going to eat it. Tonight, though, you'll just fuck it till I go crazy."

The term had eluded him; he'd never heard it before. "A bread and butter fuck?" he asked.

"Honey," she had explained patiently, "a bread and butter fuck is a straight fuck. You on top of me with my legs wrapped around you – nothing kinky... just plain old fashioned fucking. Bang, bang, thank you ma'am. Or in this case, thank you, sir!"

She bent her legs at the knees, placing her feet right up next to her buttocks. Then she spread herself for him. "Come on in... the water's lovely," she crooned, her black eyes aflame with lust, and smiling wickedly through bared teeth. Her cunt was smiling too, its dark hair-lined vaginal lips already wet with its lust, its clitoris standing proud like one of the castle's many turrets.

He entered her with a hard shove. "Gaaaagghh,"

she moaned happily as the cock rode up her vaginal passage like a non-stop express elevator until his balls slammed in against her asshole; the suddenness of his attack brought a low groan of pain-delight from his wife. Her legs uncoiled and then her calves were against his buttocks, her heels and toenails were used as spurs. She began grinding her ass into the mattress, making sharp little circular motions that were viciously exciting. He really didn't have much moving to do; she did most of it, arching her back and using her legs on his buttocks as though she were hanging from gymnastic rings. She was the master of the moment; she was the director, star, manager, boss. His hot penile shaft drove into the target, and with each new thrust, her open pussy became juicier and even the very quick of her seemed hotter. His wife was lying there – taking it all... breathing heavily through her flaring nostrils. "Slowly," she commanded, and it was a definite order, not to be disobeyed.

Suddenly there was a shimmering of consciousness, and a strange heat was on him. Always he had tried to be gentle, if possible. He didn't like the queenly attitude of his wife. Now for some sadistic reason that only vaguely made sense to him, he wanted her to know that there was only one boss at a time like this – the male! Actually, he wanted to hear her submit completely and actually plead for mercy. He withdrew his cock until only the head was still buried in the vaginal folds. His wife looked up angrily and said. "Keep going, you fool. I said, 'slowly', not stop."

He grinned down at her, then shoved forward as viciously as he could.

"Aaaa... gaaaaahhh!" she screamed, and he knew he was hurting her – knew he was scraping and rattling like a runaway subway train along each dark bend and curve of her vaginal tunnel. He felt his cock abruptly slap up against her cervix. He immediately withdrew it once more and slammed all its nine-inch length into the covering hole. "Oh fuck," the woman moaned, "I said take it easy; you're hurting me." Now Bill felt as though he were a human pile driver. He had a massive steel beam which had to be driven through that quivering quicksand into bedrock. He began driving in – without pity – hearing her groan and moan beneath him. Once, their pelvises crashed together so hard that he was sure he had broken something. His prick had grown to astronomical size; it was as if it had a mind of its own – a predatory destroyer rampaging through the warm jungles of her defenceless cunt.

Bill glanced down at the female. Her mouth was laxly open, and her breath was hissing through bared teeth. She was rotating her shoulders as though she were trying to take wing and fly. She was panting... and her eyes were rolling wildly. She seemed very close to coming. Well, fuck it!

With sadistic pleasure, Bill withdrew his cock completely. Her haunches rose up like a blind animal, weaving in the air, seeking it. "What's... what's wrong?" she panted. "Don't stop now... you

can't stop."

"Why not?" he growled, wanting only to hear her beg.

She guessed his purpose. "You fucking, impudent, little bastard... fuck me!" she hissed, and then grabbed his testicles and yanked so hard it felt as though they were being ripped out by the roots. Her fingernails cruelly and purposely dug into the scrotum.

Bill reacted much the same as a bull being pricked by a picador. He charged! "Why you... you!" He savagely slapped her face. Her head flew back against the pillow; her eyes glazed from the blow. The pain in his balls was agonizing. He wanted only to punish the bitch now.

He wanted to hurt her more that he had ever wanted to hurt anyone before in his life.

He put his steel-hard cock against her tender vaginal mouth and shoved; as he did so, he pushed her knees back until her face peered between them like . It gave him another two inches of depth, and she screamed in genuine pain as he reached the virginal territory.

In and out he drove with demented fury, a fury that did not die even when she screamed, "I'm coming. Fuck harder, you Yankie bastard. I'm coming!" Her loins were trying to work up and down on his shaft, but he kept her pinned there. She groaned and fell back – no longer fighting him as her orgasm began. He could feel her pussy twitching and sucking away at him, could feel the sudden new heat of her steaming snatch as her cum flooded her hidden passageways. He kept pounding mindlessly into her until she screamed a minute later, "I'm coming again... ohhhhhhh!" This was followed within seconds by another cry of release, then another, then still another, until her orgasms began running together in one continuous aurora borealis of ecstasy glowing and dancing across her wildly clamping pussy walls. Finally, her eyes rolled into her head and she passed out completely. Bill, propped up by knees and elbows, glanced down at her. He pinched her nipple; she remained unconscious. Then, grinning sardonically, he made one – two – three savage thrusts forward before his cock began spurting its scalding hot cum directly against the hot, still slightly pulsating walls of her passive cunt. God how he had come! It was the come of a conqueror fucking a helpless female captive... a slave of lust... the come of hatred and mastery... but not of love.

He fell alongside her unconscious body and gave way to a victorious sleep.

Some time later in the dream, he vaguely recalled her voice sleepily saying, "That was the best fuck I've had in years. Simply years, darling. But you were a very bad boy. You hurt me. You've really made me quite sore... but I'll forgive you, you loveable, uncontrollable bastard."

And still later, the voice said, "Repeat after me. At two o'clock tomorrow night, you will come to me again. Now, you will return to your room and when you awake tomorrow morning, it will all seem like a dream. It will have been a dream – you made love to your wife..."

Just before final oblivion came, he thought he heard her laughter and thought he caught the words, "Tomorrow night, my dear, I'll not let you off the leash like tonight. Tomorrow you are going down between my legs and eat it..."

What a screwy dream! Really wild! As if his bride would ever talk or act like this. Quietly, so that he wouldn't disturb Jenny, he got out of bed and went to the shower.

As he stepped under the stream of hot water, he laughed and said aloud, "I feel listless, man, almost as if I really had been screwing all night." Then almost immediately he thought: A helluva thing – having a wet dream on my honeymoon; that doesn't speak too much of Jenny's love-making abilities. He felt a trifle guilty when he realized that the dream probably was based on wishful thinking – based on the hope that Jenny would start showing some emotion, some initiative, and would relax and enjoy his love making.

It wasn't until he was towelling himself dry that he noted the very slight bruise on his right calf. It looked almost as if he had pricked himself with a pin or something.

CHAPTER SEVEN

When he arrived shortly after lunch, Jenny was fascinated by Lord Drymuir. A real earl! He's charming, she thought, but a strong wind would blow him away. He was shorter than she was and seemed rather old in appearance but young in action. His manners were so nice, so polished... and he even wore a bow tie and had a very small rosebud boutonniere on the lapel of his tweed suit. He had bowed low, kissed her hand, and told her she was 'charming' and 'delightful'.

Lady Liza Huntly, his younger sister, was something else again. She frightened Jenny by the almost intrusive intensity of her stare. By contrast, she was tall and though she had a magnificent bosom, her shoulders were broad and square. Her hair was grey and cut like a man's, and she wore a no-nonsense tweed suit. When Lady Liza spoke, her voice was nearly a baritone and it purred like a hungry tiger shortly before feeding time. In a great many respects, Jenny thought, Lady Liza looks and acts an awful lot like the girl's physical education teacher back home who was fired after some scandal involving two freshmen year girls and another teacher. She had been told that the aristocratic woman had once been somebody's bride, but the marriage had not been a success, ending in divorce.

However, in Bill's mind, there was no doubt whatsoever. Lady Liza was a card-carrying, fully-paid-up member of the Diesel Dykes' Union, a butch type if he had ever seen one, and he wasn't about to let his naive wife stumble into a situation where she would have to defend herself. As for Lord Drymuir, that was something else again. Bill had noted that the older man was sizing him up; it was almost as if he were an old stallion looking at a young stud as possible competition. The McAlisters obviously liked their cousins. Indeed, for just a brief moment he thought he had glimpsed an intimate flash between Mary and Lord Drymuir, but then he mentally laughed. "Besides," Bill told himself, "the poor old bastard probably hasn't had a hard-on since before World War II." He couldn't imagine the old goat and Mary together. He could imagine himself with her, however. The image was exciting, and once again he saw himself in the dream with her. Mary seemed somehow different this morning – a healthier glow, an air of contentment. As far as that was concerned, even Jenny seemed more relaxed – different – this morning. He couldn't quite put his finger on the difference; it had to be, he thought, because she had finally had a good night's sleep.

Bill listened to the four older people gossip about obviously wealthy and important friends. It was pretty boring stuff, especially so considering that it was such a beautiful afternoon... a day to be outside, not inside yakking inside the castle, however quaint or interesting it was. He glanced at Jenny and raised his eyebrows questioningly. She nodded imperceptibly. Bill stood and apologized, "I hope you'll forgive us; we have a date to go sailing this afternoon."

"Of course, of course," Lord Drymuir said. "Shall we meet for cocktails?"

"We'd be honoured, sir."

Jenny ran upstairs to change into shorts and a sweater, while Bill went out to the dock and unfurled the small sail on the boat. Jenny was back again within five minutes, and a short time later they were rapidly skimming across the loch.

Back at the castle, McAlister had shown Lord Drymuir to his room. The two cousins stood at the window watching as the boat sailed around a point of land and disappeared from sight.

"By Jove, the girl's really something," George Drymuir said admiringly, as he laid down the binoculars he had been using to study Jenny's breasts and legs.

McAlister snorted. "You don't know the half of it."

"Why you wicked devil you. I suppose you've already sampled the merchandise."

"Merely my official duties as taster to the head of the family."

"And how did it taste?"

"All honey, m'lord," he laughed.

Lord Drymuir cocked one eyebrow in amusement. "I don't suppose you stopped with that. A bit of buggery for dessert, perhaps? How was that?"

McAlister stopped smiling. He stared at him and said with great sincerity, "Incredible. Absolutely incredible! She has the most phenomenally talented rectal reactions of any apprentice I have ever met. The first time, the very first time she's ever indulged, and already she reacts like a specialist."

"Come now, Johnny. She can't be all that good."

"She is! Furthermore, she's so innocent, so naive, that one would almost suspect she's acting."

"Perhaps she is."

"No, she isn't putting on." He paused, thoughtful. "I really suppose I should try to cure her vaginismus before we start our training sessions."

Lord Drymuir looked alarmed. "I say! Is it contagious?"

McAlister guffawed. "No. It's just the silly little bitch thinks sexual intercourse is painful to her. She's been brainwashed by someone. Her wretched, Bible-belt mother, probably."

"Well, it's our Christian and charitable duty to do all we can to bring joy to her life," Lord Drymuir said, with a cunning, vulpine smile.

McAlister's stare was enigmatic. "She has a great deal of joy already, providing she can learn to relax."

"What is that supposed to mean?"

"Brace yourself. I know this will come as a traumatic shock. The boy could loan you a couple of inches and he'd never miss it."

Lord Drymuir glared. "That's supposed to be a joke?"

"No. The truth. You might ask Mary. He went in so deep that Mary was walking bow-legged twelve hours after the event."

"I don't believe it!"

McAlister shrugged. "You'll have your chance to see him in action with Mary tonight... after our photographs are taken."

Lord Drymuir still looked irritated when McAlister left him ten minutes later. He went to the window and noticed that the boat had come into sight again beyond the headland. His mouth watered as he though of the enjoyment to come to him tonight and the delights – the sheer delights – that would come tomorrow when the girl would be forced to do anything he asked.

Aboard the boat, Jenny watched Bill expertly tacking against the wind. She sat on a big red flotation cushion, which also served as a lifebuoy in case of capsizing. How sure he seemed of himself, she thought. How very poised for a young man, and how very handsome! She was so proud of him. She shifted her buttocks against the cushion, seeking a more comfortable position. That dream last night! That had been quite a dream – so real! Moreover, this morning she had even awakened with her anus feeling rather sore. She supposed the soreness had something to do with the breaking of her hymen. Her vagina still ached... odd about that part of the dream, too. She felt a vague stirring of excitement as she remembered Bill's tongue and lips down there in her dream. She resolutely told herself that it was Bill in the dream, even though he had McAlister's features. That coupled with Bill's making love to her in her bottom! Men didn't do that with women... or did they? She wished life was that simple – that men and women could just make love any old way they wanted and enjoy it. Perhaps some did. In her case she knew it was wishful thinking anyway. She wasn't normal; she knew it now. It was all well and good to have a dream where you reached a climax two different ways, but reality was a different thing... and reality had already proven that her mother was right: Jenny was physically unable to enjoy normal sexual intercourse because of the pain.

Abruptly she stiffened as she recalled another part of the dream. Again, in her mind, she heard the phrases, "mental vaginismus" and "monosymptomatic hysteria." Now where did I ever learn crazy words like that, she wondered.

"Penny," Bill said.

"Who?"

"A penny for your thoughts."

Jenny smiled and impulsively wrapped her arms around his outstretched legs. "I was just thinking how lucky I am... with you as my husband." It was the truth, and she knew it.

Bill kissed the top of her head, then pointed to a small beach at the foot of one of the hills; it was hidden from the castle and from other viewpoints. "What say we picnic – go swimming here tomorrow?"

The beach did look terribly inviting. "Oh, honey. Can we?"

"I don't see why not. They told us the loch belonged to the castle grounds." He leered at her, and one eyebrow shot up suggestively. Imitating Lord Drymuir's patrician tones, he said, "We could even... ah... dispense with bathing suits. How about that?"

Even thought he was making a joke, she knew he was probably serious. "Bill! I'm surprised at you."

Her blushing protest brought laughter from him.

The afternoon wind had sprung up since they left the castle; choppy little waves slapped across the bow and sides. They both were beginning to get wet when Bill turned and began running with the wind toward home. It had taken them almost an hour and a half to reach the far end of the loch; the return trip was done in less than twenty minutes. Bill swung the tiller and the sails fluttered as the boat coasted in to dock – touching as gently as thistledown landing on grass.

"Can I help store things or anything?" Jenny asked.

Bill shook his head. "I can manage. Why don't you run on in and put on some dry clothes."

Jenny shivered. "I am getting a little chilly to tell the truth."

"Take a real hot shower then."

Jenny kissed him, and then headed toward the castle. Bill watched her buttocks jiggle inside the tight little shorts and, bringing two fingers to his lips, made a loud wolf whistle. Jenny looked back – grinning and pleased – then gave a little scream as the two dogs came racing past her towards him and jumped on board barking excitedly.

Ten minutes later, Bill completed the securing of the boat and went upstairs to their suite. "Jenny," he called, when he opened the door. There was no answer. Then he heard the water running in the shower. The mental picture of his wife, nude in a steamy shower, hit him almost immediately, and with considerable urgency. His cock started growing painfully. He tore his clothes off and left them in an untidy heap on the floor. He padded into the shower room. Jenny was singing a happy song above the sound of the water. Bill looked down at his erection, now standing out in front of him as though an inflexible pole had been driven into his midriff.

Grinning wickedly and feeling extremely aroused, he stepped into the steam-laden shower room.

Jenny had her back toward him. She had lathered herself all over, and the white soap bubbles clung lovingly to the shining pink cheeks of her firm, rounded buttocks. Very kissable, he thought.

Slowly, Bill put his hands around her and cupped both of her breasts.

She screamed and spun around, eyes wide in fright. Then she closed her eyes and sighed, "My God, how you scared me. My heart feels like it's going to pound right out of my ribcage."

"Yes. I can feel it." Bill grinned and gently squeezed her left breast.

Only then did Jenny look shocked as if she had suddenly realized where he was. "Bill, you shouldn't be... I mean..." she was flustered. He merely laughed and turned on the two other shower nozzles. Jenny could feel one of them spraying against her buttocks. It stung sensually.

She watched as Bill took the soap and began lathering himself all over. The soapy water ran in a trail from his shoulders and breasts down to the pubic hair from which the almost vertical tree-trunk of his penis projected. He seemed terribly aroused she could tell by the way he acted... in addition to his erection. And, to be honest with herself, she was feeling a bit of wicked excitement herself.

"Turn around," he ordered, "and I'll wash your back for you."

Smiling modestly, eyes downcast, Jenny did as she was instructed. She felt the roughness of the wash cloth rubbing against her upper shoulders. Then he was moving down to a spot directly in back of her breasts. She glanced down and saw that both of her nipples were erect and that her areolas were covered with foamy goose bumps. Now he was rubbing her buttocks – first roughly with the rag, then gently and lovingly with just his bare hands covered with slippery warm soap and water. She could feel the soap suds slithering down the crevice beneath her spine and abruptly she remembered the dream of being made love to that way. Bill's hands were all over her now. Breasts, buttocks, abdomen...

She felt him move back from her for a second and, feeling disappointment, she turned and saw him lathering up his penis and pubic hair. Then he was back again, his hard cock pressing against the smooth, white cheeks of her buttocks, his chest hair against her back. He kissed her shoulders, her neck, and lifted the hair from the nape of her neck and licked there. A shiver of delight went through her entire body. If her heart had been pounding before in fright, it was running away in excitement now. He pressed his prick forward into soapy buttocks. Jenny stood there, feeling the exquisite sensations of his stiff penis against the slippery cheeks of her ass. Then he slid it beneath her and it rubbed against the labia of her cunt. Immediately, she tensed. It hurt. Bill, however, was making no effort to penetrate. She looked down at her front and could see the tip of his penis protruding out from the soft curls of pubic hair between her legs. To her, it looked as if it were her own. Without volition and not really realizing what she was doing, she ran her hands down across her soapy belly, through her damp nest, and clasped the head of the cock in both hands. She squeezed. It was an electrifying thing for her; she had never touched him before, not this way, not in this manner. She could feel the current flowing between his prick and her hands. It was beautiful... it was exciting... it was the most sensual thing she had ever felt in her life – except for the silly dream, of course.

Bill felt her hands there and he groaned. God, he thought, I'm so excited I'm about to come right now. I feel like a hopped-up high school kid getting his first piece of tail and coming before he's even able to put it in. He began making little swaying movements to and fro, and his desire hardened prick slid along the entire length of her vaginal crevice – from clitoris to anus. She moaned. He wasn't sure whether it was one of pain or delight.

A moment later, when she moaned again, he knew she liked it.

He had both of his hands on her hips bones now, moving them and her away from him, then back to him. There was friction – a hot soapy glorious friction – on his cock. Friction from her vaginal lips and the soft fringe of her pubic hair, friction from the cheeks of her ass, friction, even, from the little raised pucker of her anus. Abruptly he became aware that Jenny was doing an absolutely wild and wonderful thing with the muscles of her buttocks. She was flexing them, and with each movement he made they tightened along both sides of his cock. He began moving faster and faster. He wanted to put it in her; he wanted to stick it in her cunt, her asshole – anywhere! – for he could feel the waiting load of sperm in his balls beginning to surge impatiently.

Jenny, gasping for breath, knew she wanted him inside of her bowels. She could remember the dream. She wanted him deep in her bottom! She wanted him, also, deep inside her womb! She wanted him inside her belly, no matter how it hurt. She could feel all her nerves, all her muscles, all of everything crying for release. The only release would come from him being somewhere inside of her. She turned suddenly and the hardened penis slipped from between her legs. Bill groaned. Her open mouth reached up hungrily for his lips, and she savagely kissed him in an attempt to communicate her urgency, her acquiescence, and her desire. Then, she forced her hand down to his straining cock. It took all the will power she owned to make her hand close around it. Bill groaned deep in his throat. She remembered Cindy's activities with Dan. She moved her hand experimentally on the long hard hot shaft, and could feel the skin moving – but not the shaft itself. It feels like the scruff of a puppy's neck, she thought, then excited beyond belief, she began pumping on it. Bill had begun French-kissing her, and his hands had slipped down to her buttocks. He kneaded them, and she felt the most delicious of lewd sensations.

Jenny was no longer attempting to stroke him; she was frantically pulling at that virile instrument – trying to pull it into her vagina – when Bill suddenly let out a low moan of delight and stopped breathing. The cock swelled in her hand, and then she felt it begun throbbing. She watched it, fascinated, as the white hot cum spurted out all over her belly and pubic hair; it ran in great white rivers to join the soapy trails streaming down her glistening thighs. Bill continued to come, his penis continued to throb for almost a full minute. He kept his eyes closed in rapture during the entire thing. Finally, he sighed deeply as if just beginning to breath again. She detected a faint odour of salty sea with a hint of chlorine.

"Ummmmm, that was the greatest!" he said.

Jenny blinked uncertainly, trying to assess her emotions. She was pleased that she had made him feel good; perhaps the word "pleased" wasn't strong enough. She was "happy" that she had been able to. It was her own feelings that were troubling her right now. She still felt the intolerable heat of her own desires – those strange, alien desires which she couldn't analyze. Jenny knew that there had been a shameful, uninhibited moment there when she had actually wanted to bend over in front of him and spread her buttocks apart so he could insert his penis in her rubbery anus, plunge it deep into her clasping rectum. Another moment she had felt the overwhelming need of having it – no matter how agonizing – put into her vagina. And there had been the feeling of that wonderfully strong piece of hard flesh beneath her hands... she had, when the heat had been the greatest, wanted to kiss it – to pay tribute to it. She knew now why some writers called it 'a godhead'.

She looked down at Bill's maleness. It was flaccid, now barely three or four inches long, but still oozing pearly cum and covered with soap suds. Then she threw back her head and began laughing. It was a laugh of relief, of happiness shared, of delight with the moment in time and space.

"What's wrong?" Bill asked, puzzled and feeling she was making fun of him.

Impulsively, she threw her arms around his waist and put her head against his chest. She was getting her hair all wet, and she'd have a terrible time getting it set properly before dinner tonight, but she didn't care. "I love you," she said, squeezing him. She giggled again. "You felt just like... like a dying horse... twitching away there."

A second later he was laughing with her. And abruptly Jenny knew that everything was going to be all right between them, that sex would not be painful once her vagina had stretched a little and become accustomed to his size. Nothing, absolutely nothing, could spoil their happiness, she thought with all the innocence of the young.

Within her body, the heat began building up again... and she was impatient to give her husband that accommodation as soon as possible.

CHAPTER EIGHT

Dinner and the asinine conversation seemed interminable to Mary. She had been hotly impatient for the real activities to begin after everyone went to bed. The bittersweet anticipation had made her irritable as she waited for the signal from behind the window. She kept looking up at the one-way mirror, waiting for those two impossibly slow fools to get their photograph equipment ready. Bill had started to awaken twenty minutes before, and she had been forced to tell him, "Sleep... go back to sleep... until I tell to awaken... sleep..."

After an eternity, she finally heard McAlister's disembodied voice say, "All right, Mary. Now you can have your little fun and games. Don't get so carried away that you forget to keep his head facing us."

There was a loud evil chuckle from Lord Drymuir, who said, "And don't forget to say cheese."

Mary threw a withering look at the mirror, then began crooning, "Bill... wake up, darling... you are with your wife..."

Mary watched him as he began stirring. My God, she thought, I've never been so on fire before over a male. The boy was so young, so virile, so very masterful. And that cock of his – simply bull-like, with the balls to go along with it. Really, it belongs in some great museum alongside other superb world-class sculptures.

Mary's impatience had been building all day, and she had been in a state of complete arousal since early this morning. The knowledge of what she was going to make him do to her, together with what had happened between Lady Liza and the new maid, had caused both her libido and emotions to run away with her.

Earlier, having lured Mary to her room on some pretext or other and after making her usual unsuccessful sexual advances, Lady Liza had asked about the possibility of a young girl. Mary had replied there was one, Morag, a new maid especially hired for the occasion.

Mary said, "Morag's just eighteen. She's no virgin – not for your purposes, and certainly not from a male standpoint. I have a feeling she rather enjoys it any way she can get it. She came to us from a girl's reform school in Aberdeen. Left when some sort of scandal occurred."

"Scandal?" Lady Liza had arched her eyebrows hopefully.

Mary pursed her lips, then grinned. "Five girls. A daisy chain."

"And she was one of them?" Lady Liza's eyes were glowing with an unholy fire.

Mary nodded and waited a moment before dropping the bombshell, "Morag was... the ring... or should I say 'chain-'... leader."

"Where is she? I must have her, immediately. Send her to me. Quickly." The older woman was almost salivating now, her eyes glittering with a kind of obscene excitement.

Mary picked up the telephone and called down to the kitchen to ask that the new girl be sent up with some tea for Lady Liza. Then she made her way through the secret passageway to a viewpoint above the room.

Although Mary was not by nature a lesbian and derived only minor enjoyment from participation, she always found it exciting to watch women working on each other. And this afternoon's episode had been very exciting.

It had been perfectly obvious that Lady Liza terrified the young maid. She looked like some poor little rabbit suddenly thrust into a cage with a hungry ferret. She stood silently trembling with fear as the older woman made outrageous advances to her. Yet, it was not until Lady Liza had attempted to zip down the girl's uniform that the maid tried to escape. She got a sharp slap for her pains.

"You little idiot! Do you want me to tell your mistress about that disgraceful episode in Aberdeen?" Lady Liza shouted, her face red with anger.

Morag wilted right on the spot. "Oh, Ma'am,

how could you know about that?"

"I know about a great many things. Well, don't haver, you stupid girl. Answer me. Are you to let me be nice to you and reward you with a gift of money later – or am I to report you to your employers, and have you sacked without reference?"

The girl had not answered, but her head lowered and her shoulders slumped. She nodded.

Lady Liza grinned in triumph, then slowly began to undress the girl. She exclaimed over and kissed every feature of the girl, from the freckled tight little breasts to the large white hips and full buttocks. She almost went wild when the Morag's soft red pubic hair and prominent mound of Venus was finally uncovered. The older woman had forced the girl to undress her, then Lady Liza shoved the maid's body back until her hips were on the bed. She eagerly pulled the girl's legs apart.

From her vantage point, Mary had just been able to hear Lady Liza's excited gasp of pleasure as she peered between the girl's open thighs. Then Mary saw what it was that had thrilled Lady Liza so much. Morag's clitoris! It was the size and shape of a shelled Brazil nut – just as thick, and a bit longer. It was fully erect now, and Lady Liza lost no time in clamping her hungry mouth and lips over it. The young redhead had squealed like a stuck pig. Furthermore, she had come within seconds and had flooded the wildly sucking woman's mouth with a cream thicker than honey. She continued to orgasm as Lady Liza's educated tongue and fingers wreaked a divine havoc with her sensitive clitoris and labia. The girl lay there helpless in desire and panting as the older woman moved the girl's legs onto the bed, straddled her, then lowered her own dripping cuntal lips to the girl's wide open mouth. In a sixty-nine position, the maid ate hungrily, even eagerly, as Lady Liza redoubled her efforts at young Morag's tender crotch. They both had screamed out their climaxes, the sweat had poured off their thrashing bodies, and their eyes rolled back and forth in a frenzy of passion-fuelled sexual ardour.

Somewhere during this, it was obvious to Mary that the maid was beginning to obtain control over the butch dyke. It was the girl who began directing operations, and it was she who – timidly at first, and then with increasing vigour – wormed a finger up the tight anal opening between Lady Liza's broad white buttocks. The older woman had groaned in surprise, but a moment later was mewling in ecstasy as a second and third finger joined the first in a frenzy of anal fingering.

And so it had gone for almost fifteen minutes. Lady Liza had finally called for a halt. Painting in exhaustion, she directed the still eager girl to a suitcase and told her to pull out an expensively tooled leather box. The box was opened and the girl, her eyes wide in surprise and admiration, reverently pulled out an ten-inch dildo from which two large inflatable balls dangled. Mary continued to watch as the maid was instructed to fill the balls with warm water. When the dildo was strapped on, the girl went to work like a maniac on the older woman who crouched on her hands and knees, her generous bottom thrusting back every time the girl slammed the dildo into her.

"And now your Ladyship, would you like my big prick up your arse?" asked Morag with as much irreverence as she could possibly muster.

"Yes, yes... put it in..." Lady Huntly panted. "Be gentle... please?"

But Morag was anything but gentle. She derived a great deal of pleasure from watching the huge dildo sink into the big woman's tight anal ring, and she started to bugger the older woman mercilessly. Lady Huntly dived her hand between her thighs in order to extract as much physical pleasure from this as she could. As her busy fingers sought out, and found, her clitoris, she reflected upon the exquisitely ironic nature of her current humiliation – being buggered by a mere chit of a girl, and a serving-girl at that!

The sight was too much for Mary; she had begun rubbing her own wet pussy before gasping and running from the room. She couldn't watch it any longer. If she'd found Bill at that moment she would have raped him on the spot. The big dildo, strapped around the young redheaded maid's crotch, seemed to her an urgent reminder of Bill's mammoth tool. It was almost the same size as the dildo; but more importantly, it was real! A real prick on a real man! And now, in her imagination she could once again feel it smashing into her pelvis once again like a pile driver.

Mary's blood continued to boil all through tea,

cocktails, and dinner. It was all she could do to keep from reaching over under the table and grabbing Bill's genitals. He would have been surprised, she thought. Surprised and no doubt pleased.

But now her long impatience had come to an end with the signal that the photographers were ready. She knew her vagina was seeping – it had been since earlier in the day – and was lubricated to the point where she could take him easily. First, though, there were the pictures to be considered. She nodded up toward the two-way mirror, then turned to the sleeping boy. "Bill... wake up... you are with your wife."

Bill's legs twitched twice, then he yawned and opened his eyes. He blinked.

"Hello, darling," Mary said, and threw back the covers so that both of their nude bodies could be photographed.

"Hello... Jenny?"

"Bill, kiss me."

The boy moved next to the woman's mature body; she strained her breasts toward him. They lay side by side facing each other as he took her in his arms and kissed her. She threw one leg over his thigh and rubbed her thick pubic bush against his still sleeping cock. It, too, came awake – terrifyingly so. She knew the photographs would be splendid, and so now she prepared him for the really candid shots.

She pulled her mouth away from his and forced him to turn over on his back. She began kissing him as she slowly drew a line with her tongue down across his chest, past the belly button, until she reached the pubic forest where one huge tree grew to enormous height. She clamped her lips over it and was rewarded with a low moan of pleasure. She kept her mouth there until she was sure the photograph had been taken. Then she gave him a little nibble or two and used her tongue to tease the head – just as a reward. He moaned with each new thing she did.

Mary finally looked up at him. "Did that feel good, dear?"

He moaned his assent.

"Don't be selfish then. Do it to me, too." She moved herself around until her head was pointing toward the mirror, then spread her legs in open invitation to his mouth to feast upon.

Bill looked uncertain – not unwilling to participate – more as though he were unsure of exactly what to do. Mary said, "Don't be bashful. I'll tell you how to do it."

He moved directly to her open vagina. He kissed it awkwardly. She half sat up and used her fingers to pull vaginal lips apart. "This," she said, tapping the protruding little knob, "is the clitoris. It is the most sensitive part of a woman's body. A kiss there is sensual beyond description. A sucking or slight nibble there is totally devastating in its beauty. A chewing motion on the labia is enough to make any woman insane with joy. Your tongue fluttering like a frightened bird in the vagina itself will put me in absolute delirium." She lay back allowing the sensations to wash over her like high tides at

the equinox. He was understandably awkward at first, but then his dexterity and sureness grew as his tongue and lips accustomed themselves to their strange duties. She could feel herself building up to a climax as he licked away at her cunt. Then, abruptly, she remembered the photographs. "Stop," she ordered. Like a robot, he did as was directed.

She twisted around until her head was on the pillows. "Bill, let's do it together. Turn around, dear." She guided his ass with her hands until his buttocks were above her head, his face poised directly above her widespread pussy. She slowly opened her legs and, at the same time, used her hands to pull his hips and giant cock down to her mouth. She lowered it to her like an oil well drill being put into the test hole. She kissed it reverently, then teased its knob with her teeth. Bill, meanwhile, eagerly went back to work using his tongue against her cunt. Despite all of her good intentions of doing everything right for the photographs, the taste of his cock in her mouth drove Mary right out of her mind. She began sucking avariciously, trying desperately to swallow its entire length... She wasn't sure what Bill was suddenly doing to her cunt that was different, but of the hundreds of men who had swirled their tongues between her thighs, she had never felt quite the same sensations before. He licked, then brutally bit, the lips; the pain was exquisite. He used his chin to agitate the clitoris; the stubble of beard on his chin was the same as sandpaper against the tiny sensitive bud. She was panting now, she didn't care what happened. She rubbed her lips around his cock and reached up and used both hands to salaciously milk his giant balls dangling like gypsy earrings on both side of her face.

Bill drove his tongue into the insatiable vagina just as viciously as he had used his prick as a reaming instrument the night before. Mary tried to lift her buttocks to meet him, but he refused to let her move. She was losing control of the situation again; he was too masterful to be kept on a leash... he had broken his leash again, she knew it the moment that it happened. "Oh, God," she moaned as he bit her buttocks with enough strength to draw blood to the surface. Down his cock slammed into her throat. She could no longer breathe. She was choking to death. He was seemingly trying to dislodge her tonsils. Using her fingernails as sharp claws, she raked the backs of his thighs in an effort to get breathing space, but it was futile. The pain merely drove his hardened rod of flesh down deeper into her aching throat. Mary knew she was helpless... helpless because of her own sensations down there. He was using her mouth as a cunt! And suddenly she was there, coming in torrents in his mouth – coming as though something had been unleashed deep inside her pussy... treasures pouring out of an unlocked box. He drove his cock down past her tonsils, and the huge head ballooned as he reached his climax. So large was the exploding head, so big was the mouthful, that Mary couldn't even swallow. She made gagging noises as the hot cream poured down her open gullet and spilled out of both sides of her mouth. It streamed in a white river across her face, and some of it even ran up her nostrils and on both sides of her nose where it flowed out hotly into her eyes and ears.

And during it all – even when her body was whipping around in the uncontrollable frenzy of her orgasm – she kept thinking and saying to herself over and over again, "Oh, my God! What's happening to me? What's happening to me? It's never felt this good before."

Finally it passed. Bill lay alongside her now; he stared up at the ceiling, unmoving and unresponding. Mary reached over to the bedside table and pulled a paper handkerchief out of a box. She began wiping her eyes and ears and face. She was a mess. Christ, he had shot all over everything. Pillow, her hair, bedspread; there was even semen dripping from the headboard of her bed. The taste of his hot cum in her mouth was warm wine and intoxicating. Her body was at peace for the moment, but she knew the peace would not last long for even now she wanted that cock lodged deep inside her neglected womb.

Well, she thought, now is the time to go into my act. She smiled, unashamedly, up toward the mirror where she knew the two men and their cameras were watching. The eagerness was beginning in her loins; it was but an intimation of the storm to come.

"Bill... When I count to ten and snap my fingers... you will awaken completely. You will not remember these instructions after you awaken. You will be completely awake and no longer under hypnotic control. You will be free to do anything you wish – leave or stay. One... two... three..." Mary finally reached "ten" and snapped her fingers. As she did so, she lay back on the bed... sobbing and shuddering.

Bill blinked. He looked at her. Suddenly, he realized where he was, and sat bolt upright in bed.

"I..." he was speechless.

"Oh, how could you, Bill? How could you be so cruel? And I was growing so fond of you... I thought you were a gentleman."

"Mary... I... I..." Quickly, he pulled the blue satin sheet up over his loins, and made an effort to cover her.

"Oh, don't talk to me, you beast."

Bill's face was wrinkled in bewilderment and something akin to fear. He put out a hand to her naked shoulder. "Mary, please! What happened? How did I get here?"

"Don't act so innocent. It's too late for that."

"I swear to you; I don't know what's going on."

She sobbed and the motion caused the sheet to fall away from her breast. Bill couldn't take his eyes from the soft resilient mound of golden flesh; the areoles about the size of honey-coloured fifty-cent pieces, the nipples standing erect like brown pill boxes. He wanted to kiss them, to tease them with the tip of his tongue... bite them until she screamed.

There was an alien taste in his mouth – musky,

feral, exciting! He swallowed and decided he liked the taste. Mary suddenly turned toward him, and the sheet slipped down even further to reveal the outline of her rib cage creating diagonal lines which pointed to her pouting navel.

Mary stared at him, and he noticed that her eyes – although slightly damp – were not as wet as he would have thought considering the amount of weeping she was doing. She continued to inspect his face, then she said, "You mean you really don't remember... anything?"

"I swear. I haven't the slightest idea."

Mary blinked and sniffed. She wiped her eyes with the backs of her hand, then propped herself up on one elbow. The motion brought her left breast up to within eight inches of his mouth, and caused the sheet to drop to the point where the first black line of her soft curly pubic hair could be seen. One buttock was uncovered and the golden mound of flesh testified that she sunbathed without a swimsuit. There was a crease of flesh where her thigh and buttock joined; the crease glistened in the light. "You came in here and turned on the lights," she said. "I thought at first you were drunk or sleep walking. You looked very strange. Then you... you..." she fell back and covered her face with her hands. "I can't tell you; it's too horrible."

"Mary, please!" It was a strangled plea for information. Good Lord, he thought, was I drunk? What's happening to me? Am I going insane?

Mary said, "You made me do such a perverted thing. You made us have... oral intercourse!"

Bill reacted as though he had been kicked in a vulnerable spot. He couldn't believe her. She was lying. She had to be lying! Why, no matter how drunk he was, that was something he'd never force on a woman. Never! And he sure as hell wouldn't go down on a broad. Well... maybe Jenny...

"You're lying," he said quietly, watching her for reaction.

"Am I?" she spat out. Mary picked up the kleenex limp with seminal juices. "What do you call this? The stuff that didn't go down my throat went over my face and hair." She threw the handkerchief at him. "That's yours," she said.

Almost as if afraid of touching it, Bill reached gingerly out toward the paper. It was cold, and wet with a sticky substance. He swallowed; as he did so, he realized what that alien taste in his mouth was – her taste! The taste of her pussy! It was true. The whole thing was true!

"Mary," he started, but she interrupted him. She had begun weeping again. "I know you don't believe me, but feel this..." She took his hand and placed it against her fevered cunt. Bill felt the dampness, and the heat. Mary kept his hand pressed there. "That's your saliva," she said and then added as if ashamed, "... and my love. I couldn't help myself. You... you made me reach an orgasm... just as you reached your climax." Then she put her face against his chest. "Oh, Bill. I'm so ashamed..."

Awkwardly, Bill patted her bare shoulder. He was all too aware of Mary's breasts pushing up against his midriff; her nipples were burning two holes into his belly. Too, when he had felt her pussy, it was as though he had made contact with a live wire. He looked down at her body lying alongside his. One leg was slightly raised. He could see the little blue veins under her skin. He could feel her hot breath against his chest, her lips close to his right nipple. Her cunt against his leg! Without wanting it to, his prick was stirring to life again, as fevered blood roared along the arteries and capillaries to bring new strength, new energy, new purpose.

Now that the first shock of waking next to Mary had begun to evaporate, he suddenly realized he was lying in bed with Mary... a nude Mary... and a nude Bill. He also realized that he badly wanted to fuck her.

At the rate his prick was growing, he'd only have seconds before she realized her danger. He put his hand on her shoulder and pushed her over on her back. She stared up at him, her lips moistened, her upper lip reddened from wiping his cum from her face. "I'm sorry, Mary."

She nodded. "What's done is done, I suppose. You degraded me. What makes it so bad, though..." she reached up and put both hands along his face and pulled him down close to her, "... what makes it so bad is that I couldn't help myself. I enjoyed it. I wanted you. Me – a married woman – and you – a married man! Can you ever forgive me?" She blinked as if she were about to weep again.

Bill felt his heart go out to the poor woman. He had forced himself on her. He had come in here

– drunk or sleep walking – and forced her to suck his cock. And here she was now, apologizing to him! He gently kissed her lips; she responded without moving.

"Mary, I don't know what happened. And that's a pity – that I don't remember. I wanted you last night... surely you must have felt it when we were in the study together. I even dreamed of you last night. I dreamed I made love to you. Forgive me, please?"

"I'm so ashamed," she repeated. "I wanted you, too, but you're just a boy. I'm old enough to be your mother... almost."

The comment about his being "just a boy" stung Bill, just as Mary had known it probably would. His cock was fully alive now and ready for any new adventure. The heat ignited in his prick and flowed upward – up the spinal cord to his brain, up the muscular paths to his heart which received the message and began pumping quantities of blood to serve the rising instrument. Bill kissed her again, and this time he pushed his tongue through her parted lips. She refused to open her mouth to him for a moment, then, groaning, she let it swim in. This citadel fallen, Bill moved his lips to her neck and worked his way to her breast. She attempted to force his head back, but then collapsed weakly and let him do his will.

Bill could feel the power growing in him. Never in his life had he ever thought he had a chance to fuck a mature woman like this. But she wanted him. She was his to do as he wanted; he could tell that by the way she acted. She was panting when his hands moved boldly across her smooth, well-tanned stomach and sought out her gently pulsating pussy. He sawed his finger for only a second; the passage was already slippery with lubricants – his earlier saliva and her cum.

Mary acted as though she were reluctant when he forced her thighs apart and got between them. "We mustn't, Bill," she sobbed believably. "We can't. This is madness."

"We are, though," he said through gritted teeth, and then, gently parting the pubic hair, he pushed the head of his cock against the labia of the moist open lips of her straining vagina.

Mary attempted to clench her legs together, but the movement was obviously half-hearted at best. "Be gentle," she pleaded, reaching down to grasp his hardened staff in her hand.

God, it had been even easier than he had thought. He kissed her and said, "I will." It was then he felt near delirium strike him down there; she was stroking his cock as she guided it directly to the opening of her cunt. Bill pressed in and his throbbing prick slid slowly and surely down into that delicious channel, where it glided like a gondola through the warm dark cuntal passage leading to her cervix. He went all the way in without pausing once; the journey took the better part of sixty seconds and Mary gasped in adolation all the time. Finally he was in as far as he could go. He deliberately flexed his cock a couple of times.

It was then that Mary went wild beneath him.

It was as though she had reached count-down zero and the rockets had been ignited. She simply took off! She was no longer the weeping victim; she was exhorting him to do his damnedest, "Fuck me; fuck me to death," she screamed, her heels locking tightly around the backs of his flexing thighs.

He gave her free reign for the first couple of minutes and was rewarded with her sudden, "Aiiiiieeeee... I'm coming." When she had quit twitching, he began his movements. He was gentle in the beginning, just as she had requested. But the soft hidden muscles of her vagina kept nibbling and sucking away at him as though she had a herd of hungry rabbits hidden somewhere inside her tight quivering belly. His tempo unconsciously speeded up. She was screaming in continuous ecstasy as he began to rotate it around a bit inside of her – making circles with his ass and then climbing high on her body to her clitoris into devastating contact with the trunk of his cock. Her hands were all over him now... first stroking his balls, then inserting a finger in his anus – it hurt at first and he groaned in protest, then it became so tremendously exciting that he reared back to get full benefit of it.

Bill was caught up in it now; the woman beat at his buttocks with her heels. She was all fire and water, fur and grit, in everything. Her fingers moved down his back muscles once as gently as butterfly wings, and the next trip they gouged holes in skin. That hurt. He wanted to punish her for that, so he slammed his cock in viciously, and was rewarded by a thin scream of pain and indignation.

She brought blood to his bottom and back for that.

He pounded into her like the white engine-driver rod of a speeding express train. He wanted to push his prick in so far that it would come out of her mouth. He knew he was filling her, filling her as though he were the lost piece of a mammoth jig-saw puzzle. It was wonderful... beautiful. She gasped out lewd exciting words at him at the apex of each stroke. Usually it was an obscenity and a command at the same time. "Fuck me... harder... fuck," she chanted, gasping and wheezing as though she were about to expire.

Finally her eyes grew wide in supplication. "I'm coming," she moaned. She panted and writhed. His cock was a voracious animal now, insatiable, demanding. He began using his leg muscles to propel it in even deeper, bringing moans of sheer desire and passion from the woman beneath him. She was all women of the whole world wrapped up in one woman; all women wailing and screaming and writhing as they all came at once. "I'm coming," she screamed again and again, and her fingernails dug like plows into the furrows of his back.

And Bill was coming – coming with her, coming into all the women of all the world – everyone and everything, sun, moon, and stars – all coming at once. The happiness of the women could not be denied. She was all women – he was fucking all women. She was the Goddess of cunt, he the God of the cock. She screamed and collapsed twitching beneath him and he continued to pound into her until he knew there was nothing left in his body.

The witch inside her had sucked his soul out of that tiny opening at the head of his prick.

It was a long time before he pulled the flaccid cock from her. It made a lewd, wet sucking sound as it popped out. Mary's body was soaking with perspiration. She looked at him through heavy-lidded eyes. "That was beautiful," she said in obvious dismissal. "But you'd better get back to your room." She pulled up the sheet as if hiding her body in shame from him... or bringing down the curtain on the first act.

Bill saw his pajamas lying in a heap on the floor. Feeling foolish, he began to dress. When he looked toward the bed, Mary was already asleep.

He slowly made his way from the room. As he walked the darkened hallways toward his own suite, he suddenly felt a great wave of guilt wash over him. He had betrayed his wife on their honeymoon. The guilt was compounded by the fact that he knew he would fuck Mary again if he were given half a chance... and he rather suspected and hoped that the chances would be many during the next two weeks.

CHAPTER NINE

Jenny was troubled. Her thoughts and emotions were elusive as the brown trout that swam in the dark pools of brown, peat-stained water in the river by the castle. Something was wrong! She didn't know what it was – but something definitely was not right.

Earlier that next morning she had awakened and stretched languorously, feeling more relaxed and happy than she could remember. She had been awake for only seconds before the dream returned. Once again she had dreamed that Bill had made love to her – a violent, satisfying, and thoroughly enjoyable love! And she had reached orgasm after orgasm until her climaxes had all run together in one sweet, never-ending symphony of sensation. She swallowed noisily as she remembered the details of that dream. It had been Bill in the dream, but Bill looked different... actually Bill looked more like either John McAlister or Lord Drymuir. She remembered what she had done. After Bill had licked her down there and driven her to the point of madness, he had asked her to suck on his penis. She had done so – at first out of love, but then with a deep animalistic desire to devour it. He had ejaculated into her mouth, and so entranced had she been with him that he had actually been forced to push her mouth away after she had swallowed all of him and continued to lick and suck his deflated penis. That had been the Bill who looked like Lord Drymuir. Next, the Bill who looked like John McAlister had made love to her the same way he had in the dream the night before... slamming in and out of her rectum until she was a screaming, helpless piece of wild flesh impaled like a wriggling fish on the end of some great spike. Then Lord-Drymuir-faced-Bill had made love to her in the vagina! It was this method that had caused her to reach peak after peak of progressively greater orgasms.

And through it all there had been the lightning storm – brilliant flashes of light.

These dreams surely must be the subconscious telling me that I must give myself completely to Bill, she thought. I'll tell myself that if it doesn't hurt in the dream, then it won't hurt during the real thing. She had wanted him in there during the shower yesterday; she supposed that was why she had dreamed. All the same, it was very peculiar. She felt sure she wasn't really interested sexually in Lord Drymuir or John McAlister, and so she was puzzled by the fact that her husband had their faces in her dreams.

All morning long she worried over her dream like a dog with a bone. However, at breakfast, other things happened that caused her additional alarm or concern. Lord Drymuir actually leered at her; it seemed almost as if he knew that she had dreamed about him last night. And Bill and Mary seemed to be silently speaking to each other across the table; she didn't like the hungry look on Mary's face, nor did she care for Bill's guilty glances in the older woman's direction... it was as though the two of them were sharing some secret. She felt a pang of jealousy, which she quickly dismissed, telling herself she was being silly and fanciful.

But still there was the nagging feeling that something was wrong, that the music of the days was being played off-key. Her suspicions were not relieved when McAlister, smelling of something like vinegar, arrived late for breakfast. He smiled fondly at Jenny, as if he were especially proud of something she had done. She was forced to turn her head away because she remembered that her husband had looked like McAlister when he made love in her behind during the dream.

Lord Drymuir had demanded impatiently of McAlister, "Well?"

McAlister smiled. "Perfect!"

"Even mine?" Lord Drymuir asked hopefully.

McAlister lifted one eyebrow and smirked. "Every exposure is perfect." He put a particularly nasty emphasis on the word "exposure."

Jenny noticed that Lord Drymuir and Mary both sat back, relaxed. Both had smug expressions on their faces.

Later, when she and Bill had been walking around the castle grounds, Jenny said, "Our hosts gave me the creeps this morning."

Bill, who had been pondering Lord Drymuir's and John's behavior, confessed himself equally puzzled. Actually, he was glad to have Jenny voice her suspicions. During breakfast he hadn't been sure that it wasn't his own nerves reacting to a guilty conscience. He could be honest with himself. He knew that it was really Jenny he wanted; he would do anything for Jenny. But he also wanted excitement – action and reaction. Jenny, the times he made love to her, had lain there like a big sack of potatoes. Her only comments being, "You're hurting me." Mary? My God, that was really something. How could he have gone down on her and made her blow him? He didn't doubt that it had happened... all he knew for sure was that he had dreamed he was eating Jenny's pussy... then had awakened to find himself with Mary. The dream that first night had triggered it, he thought.

The day passed leisurely. A fierce wind had sprung up over the loch, which made sailing a bit risky, so he and Jenny had taken a long hike. She seemed strangely withdrawn... he hoped she didn't sense that he had been unfaithful to her. God, anything was possible! Maybe she could smell Mary's cuntal juices on him when he returned to bed... although she seemed to be sleeping so soundly that she looked drugged.

Earlier when he had been making plans for the afternoon, he had wanted to steer Jenny to one of the deserted coves and beaches on the loch and make love to her. Now she seemed so introspective that he decided to wait until they returned to the castle. Twice she had turned to him as if to say or ask something, but then her resolute expression had changed and she turned away from him. The only crowning thing – the only thing that made him feel Jenny's problem did not include him – was her impulsive grab around his waist and her upturned face saying, "I love you, my husband!"

They had reached the castle gate when Bill found a small brown lizard sitting on a rock beside the trail. He picked it up and Jenny squealed in a little girl's fright. He held it out to her, and she squealed again. She ran. He chased her, laughing.

The dogs joined them – both barking in joyous excitement.

"Bill, don't," she screamed, running across the lawn with the dogs in pursuit.

Suddenly they all blundered into McAlister who was standing there with an amused expression on his face. Bill immediately dropped the lizard and looked as if he couldn't understand why Jenny was fleeing from him.

Jenny stood behind McAlister and peered around his shoulder at her husband. "Did you drop it?" she demanded.

In answer, Bill merely held his hands out, palms up.

McAlister grinned down at her. "I regret to say that your pet was just eaten by Regina." He nodded toward one of the hounds.

"Eeecccck," Jenny said in mock dismay.

They all three laughed. The strain of the morning was gone now. McAlister seemed genuinely pleased to see them, and she was glad to see him.

McAlister said to Bill, "Are you prepared for our twilight wild boar hunt? The beasts are specially imported for the occasion as it's not a common sport in Scotland yet."

"Tonight?"

"A good night for it. The moon will be right, and I have the Castle's ghillies, Ian and Jock, both standing by."

Bill looked at Jenny, mutely asking permission.

"Go ahead, darling," she smiled. "I'll be fine. Anyway, I have a lot of letters and cards to write."

Bill nodded. "I'm ready anytime you are, John."

McAlister clapped him on the back. "Splendid. We'll make a box lunch and take a bottle of wine... and a wee bottle of single malt. Dress warmly because it gets cold after dark. Meet you outside the garage in twenty minutes?"

"Right."

Bill was eager for the outing. Wild boar would be an excitingly different change from deer and ducks. He supposed the techniques weren't too different than those used in deer hunting... downwind, aim for the neck, make sure the first shot counts.

"We should find the herd near the oaks," McAlister told him later as they drove through the very late afternoon's sunshine toward a wooded area. "The acorns have started to fall; the pigs will be rooting around for them. Now, just one word of caution, Bill m'lad. Don't get too close. If one of them comes at you, climb a tree. You can't outrun them. The dogs will do their best to draw the pig from you, but don't count on too much from them. They've both learned their lessons about boars... the hard way. So they're a bit shy, you might say."

The sun had set beyond the hills and the sky was turning a darker blue as Bill got out of the car. McAlister said, "We're heading toward the far end of the copse to drive the pigs toward you. And please, my friend, if you hear something moving in the bushes, make sure it isn't one of the dogs... or me, especially before you blast away."

Bill nodded his understanding. A moment later

he was left all alone in the gloaming. He noticed the wind was blowing out of the west, so he cut at an oblique angle toward the woods, knowing he could approach without the pigs getting scent of him.

In the distance he thought he heard the far-off sound of dogs in front of him and McAlister's car somewhere in back of him... that, though, was impossible; McAlister was in front of him. It was then that he realized he had no idea whatsoever of where he was or, if he got separated from the hunting party, how he would go about making his way back to the castle.

"McAlister has had a lot of experiences with these twilight hunts," he said to himself. "He knows what to do if I get lost."

McAlister, indeed, knew what to do, and he was doing it as though the Devil himself was pursuing him. He drove rapidly through the gathering night back toward the castle and his long awaited subjugation of a fully conscious Jenny and her darling little anus.

CHAPTER TEN

With Bill gone, Jenny decided to have dinner by herself in their suite. Young Morag, the pretty, redheaded young housemaid, brought up the meal. She looked exhausted – almost as if she'd had no sleep for a couple of days. Jenny felt a trifle guilty about causing extra work for the poor girl and decided to make sure that Bill gave her an extra large tip when they left. She ate the solitary meal then changed into a long powder-blue silk dressing gown and a blue lace peignoir. The feeling of silk against her bare skin was wickedly exciting: suddenly she wished Bill were here.

She had sat down at the window writing desk and had begun writing a long chatty letter to Cindy when there was a knock on the door. "Come in," she called, thinking it was the maid returning for the dinner dishes.

"Good evening, my dear," Lord Drymuir said, coming in and closing the door behind him. He stood there for a moment, staring appreciatively at her gown, then walked over purposefully to the table in front of the fireplace and placed a large manila envelope upon it.

She felt a flutter of unease run through her mind. Lord Drymuir had walked in as though he owned the place. Well, to some extent, she supposed, he did own the place. No, it was more the superior, almost proprietary, manner in which he now gazed at her. It was more as if he owned her...Vaguely she felt that it was not right that he should be in a closed room with her when her husband was absent, especially with her dressed as revealingly as she was.

"Writing letters, I see," he observed, rather unnecessarily.

"Yes. To a few friends back home. Mother. Cousin... you know."

Lord Drymuir moved over right next to her

writing table. His bold eyes fastened on her gown which was open enough to see the first proud swelling promise of her breasts. Blushing furiously, she nervously put her hand up there and fumbled the peignoir's button in an effort to close it.

"That really isn't necessary, my dear. You have charming breasts. There's no need to hide them."

"Lord Drymuir! Really!" Jenny was shocked. She sputtered almost incoherently when she was his leering expression. "I think, sir, you had better leave. As you know, my husband isn't here."

Lord Drymuir's derisive laughter cut into her like a whip. Then his expression became coldly cruel. "Leave? Leave! I have no intention of leaving until I get what I came for." He boldly placed his blue-veined, age-spotted hand on her shoulder and squeezed.

Suddenly Jenny was frightened, really frightened. Lord Drymuir must be a madman! He was looking in ill-concealed lust at her breasts and at her pelvic area. "I... I... you really must go, Lord Drymuir." She stood and backed nervously away from him. His eyes were like prison yard searchlights moving up and down the length of her figure. They came to rest on a spot just below her navel – that slightly protruding spot marking her mound of Venus.

"You are quite beautiful, my dear," he said.

"Please leave."

His face suddenly became contorted in something akin to hate, and his voice was tight with anger. "Don't be impertinent! I said I would not go until I got what I came for."

Jenny walked to the door and opened it. "Get out!" she said, trying to keep her composure.

"Close the door," he demanded.

"Get out, or I shall scream."

"You may scream all you wish, but it will be of no avail. No one will hear you; the servants are gone. We are alone in the castle."

Feeling a combination of embarrassment, anger, and fear, Jenny screamed and then yelled, "Help." The echoes resounded throughout the deserted hallways, "... help... help... help." Her own voice was mocking her.

"Now that we have that silly bit of amateur theatrics out of our system, I want to show you something. Take a look at the little gift I've brought you. There, on the table... in the envelope."

"I'm not leaving this door. You make a move toward me and I'll run."

"I have no doubt that you could outrun me. It would be the most foolish thing you have done in your life, however. Take a look in the envelope. I give you my word of honour... as a gentleman... that I will not move from this spot."

Anything to get rid of this maniac, Jenny thought. She sidled over from the door toward the table, watching him closely for any movement. He merely smiled in vast amusement at her precautions. He appeared to be holding his breath, and his eyes seemed to have grown to an enormous size as he watched her unfasten the clasp on the envelope.

Jenny didn't relax her vigilance; she kept her eyes riveted upon him as she withdrew the contents. She could tell by the feel that they were photographs. She made one rapid glance down at the top one, and then room began swirling around her. She heard his awful laughter burst out, and he sat down in the chair, laughing uproariously at her stunned and disbelieving expression.

"Oh," he gasped, "if you could only see you face, my dear. Divine! Absolutely perfect! Almost as if you had suddenly stumbled upon Jack the Ripper in the darkness."

Jenny gazed down in horrified disbelief. It was a photograph of her. Not her as she saw herself each morning in the mirror, but a photograph of a totally alien her – wantonly smiling as she sucked away on Lord Drymuir's sausage-like cock. Her lips were grotesquely pouting around the instrument, but it was her expression that was the most astonishing thing about the picture. It was obvious to anyone – even herself! – that she was blissfully and erotically enjoying what she was doing. Her hands were clearly shown; one was cradling his testicles as though she were weighing them, the other had two fingers wormed deep into his anal passage.

Jenny's legs failed her. She was forced to steady herself on the back of a chair and then sink slowly into it. She continued to stare at the picture. Finally she closed her eyes and moaned, "Oh, my God!"

Lord Drymuir continued to laugh. He choked, then coughed and wheezed. "You may like to know, my dear, that no one had to tell you a thing. I have never known a more apt pupil, one who picked it up so rapidly – within seconds, so to speak. You were born to bring pleasure to a chap... and you don't have the intelligence to realize it. Pure womanly instinct." He sighed. "But really, you should look at the others."

Fear, almost wishing that God would strike her blind, Jenny turned to the next photograph. She blinked and the hot tears began streaming down her face. This picture showed her with legs spread wide apart and Lord Drymuir's head buried in her vaginal crevice. Her tongue was hanging laxly out of the corner of her mouth and her eyes were rolled back in her head. Shown clearly were her taut stomach muscles and flexed buttocks, and her fingernails clawing a bloody trail of lust down his back. Her face was smeared with what could only be cum; it glistened all over her neck, and a huge puddle of it could be seen alongside her shoulders on the rumpled sheet. As she gazed through watery eyes at the photograph, it was all coming back to her now. That dream! So it hadn't been a dream, after all. She remembered the moment; in the dream it had been so wonderful to have her husband doing that to her.

She realized that Lord Drymuir had become silent. He merely stared at her, and his expression was once again an unpleasant one... one that held something else, too.

He didn't make a command, but she turned to the next photograph... already sure of what she would see. It was a closeup of Lord Drymuir's cock in the process of being jammed into her vagina. Again, what made the picture so unbelievably horrible was the sheer look of delight and impatient lust on her face. She thought dully: It didn't hurt at all when he did that; it was wonderful. I remember the sensation now. Beautiful. But I thought it was my husband making love to me... not someone just using me, like some insensitive whore. She suddenly realized that no one seeing the photograph would ever think of her being an 'insensitive' whore. A 'whore', yes, but 'insensitive'? Never! Not with that gloating sensual expression on her face, not with those fingernails digging deeply into his driving buttocks. No, if anything, she was a very 'sensitive' whore, one who seemed to be enjoying the fuck of her life.

The next, as she was pretty sure it would, showed McAlister in the process of sodomizing her. Again the photographer had masterfully focused on her expression. She was the personification of wantonness. The hang of her proud breasts like ripe fruit about to drop from a tree, the tendons of her neck, the muscles of her inner thighs, the deep indentations created by the eager flexing of the anal muscles... all were clear indications that she was within seconds of obtaining an orgasm.

It was all too much to bear, much less understand. Her dignity crushed, sobs wracked her body and each breath was a shuddering one. She had never been so mortified, so humiliated, so ashamed in her life. The photographs, no matter how they had come to be taken, gave Jenny an insight to that darker being within her whose existence she had never known or even suspected.

Lord Drymuir was no longer amused; he stalked angrily toward the door and closed it. He stood there, impatiently rocking back and forth, glaring at her. "Whimper all you want, slut. Cry your heart out. It makes no difference. Your precious husband shall see these when he returns from the hunt tonight. And in tomorrow's post, an envelope identical to the one I gave you will be transmitted to your mother, to your local police authorities, and to..." He took his hand from behind his back and held out Jenny's blue address book. He grinned evilly "... every name in this book."

She screamed and leaped toward him; she was rewarded by a vicious backhand in the face that sent her sprawling to the rug. In falling, her peignoir ripped; her gown slithered up to her waist, where the full ripeness of her upper thighs and buttocks were fully visible to Lord Drymuir's cruelly glinting eyes. "You beast you... you filthy beast," she sobbed.

"My dear young lady. These photographs are not of a 'filthy beast'... but of a common street whore sucking, being sucked, and, being, if you'll pardon the Anglo Saxon expression, 'fucked'... and then finally being buggered. Oh, how she loves it all. Note the enjoyment upon her face. How amusing it will be when your mother and all of your little friends and relatives see what a happy honeymoon you're enjoying."

"What is it you want?" she gasped, feeling horror and sickness suddenly wash over her like an unrelenting tide of despair.

"That's hardly the question you want to ask, is it? What you really want to know is: 'How do I get those photographs back?'"

Jenny looked up from the floor. She could see the bulge growing in his trousers as he gazed at her uncovered body. She made a futile attempt to pull her gown down. A part of her mind was screaming like a frightened caged animal, "... help me, please, someone... help me." Yet she knew there would be no help. No help from the local police, and certainly none from Bill. If Bill ever saw the photographs, he would leave her in an instant. With a sudden caving in of her spirit, she asked in a barely audible voice, "What do... I have to do... to get them back?"

Lord Drymuir smiled. "Excellent, my dear. You are, as I said before, a quick on the uptake, and a fast learner." He picked up the envelope and withdrew the first one. He rolled his eyes theatrically. "Oh, yes! I remember it well. It was delightful; you showed such tremendous talent for it." He looked as if he were thinking, then nodded his head. "That's it! That seems fair enough. For each photographic scene you recreate, I shall return a picture."

As she realized what he was asking, Jenny suddenly felt a painful spasm in her stomach; she was sure she was going to vomit. Oh, God! How could any human being so degrade another, so debase another as he was trying to do to her. She wouldn't do it... she couldn't do it. She shook her head and mumbled, "I won't." Then she looked up in tearful pleading, "Please, Lord Drymuir. Please have mercy – pity. Give me the photographs. Please!" The last was a half hysterical scream.

"Of course, my child. They shall be returned to you... upon my word as a gentleman... just as soon as you fulfill the conditions of our contract."

Sobbing incoherently, Jenny shook her head violently from side to side, "I can't. I just can't do that!"

Lord Drymuir clapped his hands together in dismissal. "Then we really have nothing more to discuss. The photographs will be mailed tomorrow." He turned to the door.

"Please. Have pity." Jenny screamed.

Lord Drymuir did not answer. He opened the door and stood in the archway. "Good evening, Madam. And sweet dreams." He started to close the door.

"No," Jenny shouted in desperation and fear. "No... come back." Her body was wracked with shuddering sobs of distress, as she buried her face in her hands.

"You'll do it?" Lord Drymuir's voice was cold, inflexible.

"Oh, God forgive me... yes!" she screamed. "Yes... you, you bastard... I'll do it!"

Lord Drymuir closed the door behind him. His face was red in rage and his voice tight in poorly suppressed fury. "Watch your language, slut, or I shall have second thoughts about my generosity. As it is, you will pay a little extra for your persistent rudeness."

Abjectly, knowing she must be on his good side to get the photographs, Jenny said, "I'm sorry."

"That's better, immensely better. Now my dear, take your hands away from your pretty little face. Do it... now!" The last word cracked like a whip and Jenny's body jumped as though struck.

Lord Drymuir handed down photograph number one. "Shall we begin? Recreate this... and you may have the picture to do as you wish. Burn it, tear it, or keep it among your treasured souvenirs. Look at it closely."

"Oh, God..." she moaned in shame and distress.

"Take off your clothes." It was an order; there could be no disobedience. She rose, silent, unable to speak for the humiliation she felt. The man's eyes burned huge holes in her breasts and pelvic area. When she hesitated – hoping against hope that he would change his mind, that this was really a monstrous nightmare from which she would soon awaken – Lord Drymuir narrowed his eyes in warning. Quickly then, she took off the peignoir. Then, eyes closed and unable to look at him, she slowly lifted the gown over her head to stand naked and trembling abjectly before him.

"Beautiful, just beautiful. Now stand there until I get my clothes off." For the first time the old man began showing real signs of impatience. She watched him, horrified, as he removed his coat, tie, shirt and vest, and then unbuttoned his trousers and dropped his trousers and underpants to the floor. A moment later, he stood before her with only his shoes and socks and garters on. His huge white erection grew like a poisonous toadstool in the grey frizz of his pubic hair. "All right, my dear. Picture number one: on your hands and knees... crawl to me."

It was going to be even worse than she had thought. She kept saying over and over again in her mind, "This can't be happening to me; this can't be happening to me." Lord Drymuir was a hideous creature seen in some nightmare as he leered down at her with those horribly hot and unbending eyes. She would die before she did this. "No... I can't." She clenched her eyes tightly shut as if she could erase the scene from memory and make it cease to exist.

"If I am forced to put my clothes on, I swear to you that nothing – absolutely nothing you could offer, no matter how far you crawled – could obtain the release of these photographs. Do you quite understand?"

"Please?" she pleaded, looking at him once more in supplication. "Please..."

Lord Drymuir merely stroked his waiting cock and answered. "I'm waiting. On your hands and knees. Quickly, now!"

It was hopeless. She knew it was quite hopeless. All was lost. It didn't matter. She would die of humiliation if the photographs were released; she would die of humiliation if she were to undergo the cruel debasement in order to retrieve them. It didn't matter except... the pictures would kill Bill's love for her, would destroy her mother, would be traumatic for all her friends receiving copies. This way only she would be hurt. Slowly, she sank to her knees and began crawling like a wounded animal toward his disgusting erection.

Now all she could think about was getting horrible ordeal she faced over with as rapidly as possible. Lord Drymuir misunderstood her suddenly speeded up crawling. "Don't be so eager, my dear. You are acting as hungry as you were last night." He laughed and backed away when she reached him. She crawled forward two more paces, then reached up for his cock. He backed away again, laughing at her. "Come on," he coaxed, and moved back until his hips were against the bed. He sat down and spread his legs. Jenny could see his testicles dangling like ripe, flesh-coloured fruit above the brown puckered opening of his anus. His cock stuck up in the air at an outrageous angle, and occasionally it throbbed and jerked spasmodically.

Jenny crawled up on the platform and to the bedside, no longer conscious of moving or acting. She was merely an automated robot, incapable of independent action or thought.

"Now, my dear. For the first photograph..."

She shuddered in revulsion as she bent forward to pay unwilling homage to the waving, purple and white penis. She could see angry red veins running up its white and blue trunk and the throbbing, hooded, purple head already seeping a clear fluid. His balls were high and tight now in his purple scrotum; his greying pubic bush formed a halo around his unusually large genitalia. Inside her mind a voice kept crying out, "Ask him

once again." But she refused to heed it, knowing instinctively that it would be useless, that any abject begging and pleading on her part would only add to his sadistic enjoyment. She closed her eyes and swallowed, muttering a silent prayer, "Bill... forgive me. Please forgive me, darling, for what I'm about to do."

Her lips closed wetly about the smooth rubbery head. Lord Drymuir groaned. His eyes seared with unconcealed lust as he stared down at the top of her blonde young head. The knob of his cock tasted like sweet soap, the viscous fluid seeping from the glans was slightly saline with little or no odour. He moved the rod in her mouth. "Suck a little, nibble a little, my dear."

"I was dreaming... I am dreaming... I am dreaming," Jenny said to herself with each thrust of the hated cock in and out of her mouth. She had dreamed of doing this last night; it had been terribly exciting, terribly enjoyable... but that had been with her husband! She felt nothing now but despair and humiliation. She followed his directions, mindlessly licking and nibbling and tongue teasing as he ordered. She was sure that it would never end, but it did with Lord Drymuir's saying, "That's enough for now."

She removed her mouth from his cock. She kneeled there; head down in subjugation, waiting for whatever cruelty was to come next.

"Get on the bed," Lord Drymuir said. Spiritlessly, Jenny did as she was instructed. She lay there, legs slightly apart, staring up at the ceiling – not making any effort to cover her body. Lord Drymuir gazed speculatively down at her. "You aren't showing nearly enough enthusiasm, my dear. Perhaps we should turn that little furnace of yours up higher." He walked away from the bed and came back a moment later with the second photograph. He held it before her yes. "Shall we try for number two?" When Jenny did not answer, he slapped her with the picture. The sharp edge of the paper cut the underside of her chin, drawing a thin line of blood. "Answer me," he snarled.

"Yes..."

"Yes, what, you slut?"

"Yes. Let us do number two."

"There is a vulgarism – American, I believe called 'eating pussy'. Some of our less educated Englishmen call it 'muff diving'. Now you must ask me in a nice way – using either of those vulgarisms."

Jenny closed her eyes and sighed. "I want you to eat pussy."

"Whose?"

"Mine."

"Say it then."

She sighed again and said, without any inflection at all, "I want you to eat my pussy."

"Please?"

"Please..."

Jenny was aware that her legs were being spread apart. She flinched, in spite of herself, when his finger parted the softness of her pubic hair and touched her vaginal lips. She remembered the dream last night! Presumably Bill had been doing this to her. It had been wildly exciting and erotic beyond description. But now, she felt nothing. As he began his perverted licking, the sensations were muted, muffled, almost as if she had had a local anaesthetic administered to that part of her body. She felt a certain relief at this. But it was to be short-lived.

The numbness lasted until he reached the clitoris; he put his lips and it began sucking it as though it were a very small penis. Jenny's body stiffened as she felt the unwelcome sensations return down there. Lord Drymuir chuckled as he sensed she had finally begun to come to life. Next she felt his tongue jab into her vagina; the effect was like an electrical cattle prod. She jumped, trying to pull herself away from him. Then the slow, rhythmic, tantalizing licking began again. She flexed the muscles along her inner thighs attempting to make the unwanted feeling of pleasure go away but it only added to her enjoyment. With the tensing of her thighs, Lord Drymuir went back to lick again at the tiny pulsating clitoris.

Now Jenny was beginning to moan and sob as she realized what these sensations implied. No, this couldn't be happening to her! It mustn't happen! The nerve endings down there were betraying her. She couldn't permit this to feel pleasurable; she couldn't. But, in spite of her revulsion at the act, her abdomen rose and fell with increasing rapidity as the old man began taking long licking strokes with his tongue and using his nose to buffet the clitoris while his chin whiskers were scraping against her tightly clenched anus. She knew she was beginning to secrete lubricants and liquids from glands that were taking notice of the loving attention being bestowed them. It wasn't until she discovered her pelvis was beginning to grind lewdly into the old man's sardonically smiling face that she realized she had lost this particular battle. Her shamelessly aroused body was moving independently now, she hadn't the least control over it any longer. His hot hungry mouth enclosed the entire fleshy labial area and he began sucking voraciously at it. The exquisite sensations shot across her loins into the nerve endings at the mouth of her womb. His drooling mouth kept the labia tightly clamped, his tongue pressured its way through the compressed vaginal lip, and Jenny almost lost her mind attempting to control her reactions.

Finally – and she knew it the second that it happened – she reached the point of no return. To her disgust, she realised she was going to have an entirely involuntary climax! She fought it, screamed against it in her mind, but muscles and nerves all rebelled against the discipline – seeking instead the sweet release. Then her pelvis was jerking and her hands were trying to push the old man's face up all the way into her vagina, and a voice she had never heard before was screeching from her own throat, "I'm coming. Oh God, lick harder... faster... now... now! Uhhhhh... ohhhhhh... ohhhhh... yessssss!"

She was almost unconscious from the combination of shame and satiation when Lord Drymuir raised her knees to her chest. Abruptly she felt his penis pressing against her open, unprotected vagina.

"Now number three," he said.

"No... you'll hurt me," she moaned, but it was already too late. She attempted to scissor her legs, but the movement caused him to slip forward and his long hard cock slid effortlessly as far as the mouth of her cervix. "Gaaaagh," she screamed. God, it was excruciating. It was as if he had plunged a white-hot poker into her. Worse, far worse, more agonizing than even the first night with Bill. That pain, at least, had come from love – this came from torture and debasement and rape.

Lord Drymuir smiled down at her. "Don't put on an act, my dear." He reached over to the bedside table and pulled down the photograph. The sideways movement hurt her and she moaned in pain. "See what immense pleasure you are getting out of me. That is the real you. You're only acting right now," he said.

Jenny's eyes were blinded to the picture; the reality of the moment was that she was in pain from sexual intercourse and his huge penis. He moved it out a bit; the withdrawal motion was agonizing. He pushed it in to its utmost depth again. "Ooooohhh, God! No, please. You're hurting me. Please, I'll do anything... but not this... you're killing me." A sudden jab was the only answer to her pitiful plea. She was suddenly screaming at the top of her voice as he began viciously jabbing into her; she jerked her eyes open to see the old man's cruel sadistic grin above her. He was killing her; he wanted to hear her scream and moan; he was enjoying every second of it.

Her vagina felt as though it had shattered and was bleeding from a thousand different, places. His cock lay throbbing, sunk deep in her belly, filling every part of her insides. There wasn't a single fleshy ridge on the prick that she could not feel as it expanded tightly against the soft interior flesh of her cunt. Jenny lay immobile, afraid to move because of the pain each movement brought.

Lord Drymuir grinned down at her. He flexed his cock inside her belly and she felt it jerk up and against the cervix. "Aaaarrgggh," she groaned, and her face was twisted in pain.

Lord Drymuir merely smiled more sadistically. He flexed it again.

"Oooohhh..." She kept her stomach muscles as tight as possible, hoping she would create an intolerable pressure for him down there.

Slowly, Lord Drymuir pulled his hardened penis from her tight vaginal sheath until it was about half out, then slowly – oh, so very slowly – pushed it in again. He did this for about three minutes.

"Oooohhh, please... you're... hurting." She said it automatically, and with a sudden jolt to her brain realized that she was screaming a lie. Oh, it was tight, all right. Very tight. And she was being stretched painfully. But the slow, salacious movements were not painful! Furthermore, by the sudden look on the old man's face, she knew he was aware of her new knowledge.

"Now you must ask me to 'fuck' you."

"No... I won't. I can't. Please don't humiliate me any more. Do what you have to do and get it over with, but please don't ask me to degrade myself like that!"

Lord Drymuir continued to move his cock back and forth slowly. Jenny was aware that her vagina was making a wet, lewd sucking noise, as it slipped moistly in and out of her fully opened vagina and that too suddenly began to add to the forbidden excitement she felt coursing through her betraying body.

"You must beg," he said, insistently, "that is part of the contract. After all, each time you say 'please, stop', you're begging. So beg me to 'fuck' you." He shoved his prick forward and a shock of unwanted pleasure shot through her womb.

"Oooh, no! Please no." That, of course, would be the final straw – the ultimate in humiliation. She had maintained a tiny shred of pride because she knew she was suffering all this for Bill and her mother's sake. But to be forced to beg? That would be the end of her forever as a decent person. He had taken her self-respect, her fidelity to her husband... taken everything. She couldn't, she wouldn't give him the ultimate triumph of hearing her beg for him to force these horribly depraved indignities on her helpless body!

Lord Drymuir stopped moving with his penis half in, half out of her cunt. "Very well," he said. "A woman has other ways of begging. We shall see."

Jenny didn't understand what he was talking about, and she didn't waste time trying to figure it out because her mind was elsewhere... analyzing, calculating, evaluating. Something unwanted was happening in her vaginal area. The pain had disappeared. She wasn't even uncomfortable any longer. There was pleasant warmth there, pleasant pressure. When his penis twitched again she was astonished to find that – without volition – her own inner muscles had flexed in involuntary response, bringing a smile of ecstatic delight from him.

She fought with every bit of will power she had to keep from doing that again. She hadn't been conscious of doing it the first time; she wasn't sure how she had done it... please, please, just don't let it happen again. But it did happen, and there was a minor groan from him. It happened again... and again... and again until it seemed almost as if she had attached an automatic milking machine down there between her legs.

George Drymuir was making a slow rocking motion between her thighs. She could feel the narrow passageway to her innermost femininity being widened with each short stroke. The friction had quickly caused her vagina to run the entire spectrum of sexual arousal from cold agony to hot willing anticipation. The hot glow of passion outside was being rubbed and pushed inside; she could feel it creeping relentlessly along the vaginal walls to the tip of her uterus... a strange and wonderful glow. She fought that, too. She fought her breathing, which was becoming more shallow, more rapid. The perspiration popped out on her forehead as she fought a desperate losing battle with her pelvis after discovering it shamelessly rising to meet the downward thrust of his cock; she forced her pelvis back to the mattress. A second later, though, it had begun moving slowly upward again like an open-mouthed fish rising to the bait.

And then, as suddenly as it began, the battle was over. Jenny's body was asserting its independence from her ethics, her morals, her upbringing and her will power! The lewd flames of lust coursed salaciously through her veins, and her heart sped up its action in an effort to get the hot desire – contaminated blood into every part of her body. Her pelvis as she had feared, was the first to unleash itself. After a long struggle, it began moving up and down of its own volition on the white rod of hardened flesh – the two things moving in harmony and growing excitement. Her inner muscles went next; twitching against, massaging, and milking the cock for its entire length. One section of muscle squeezed so tightly on Lord Drymuir's prick that he groaned uncomfortably.

She was losing it. Jenny could mentally stand off and watch her body – as though she were watching the actions of a lust-crazed prostitute beneath a stranger's pounding weight. Her face was beginning to twist in an expression of unbridled desire. Her body writhed beneath him, and she made low hums of passionate encouragement with each new thrust of his prick. Her breath now was coming in puppy dog-like pants. Her legs on either side of his driving hips were moving in tiny lewd circles as though she were using a hula hoop. Suddenly, Jenny's mind which had been able to stand off and watch all this became too excited to be denied its participation. There was no longer any thought but the delicious sensation of lying beneath this man who was bringing her rapidly to a peak of glory she had never consciously known existed. She was coming again; she knew it. She wanted it... she didn't want it... she wanted it... she wanted it... and she was close, close, close!

Then, Lord Drymuir stopped.

Unbelievingly she looked up at him. He grinned down at her. "You do like to be fucked, don't you, my dear?"

She stared at him, burning hatred in her eyes, her nostrils quivering with each short breath she took.

He flexed his cock deep inside her.

"Ummm," she mewled.

"You like to be fucked?" He flexed it twice.

"Oh, God, help me. Yes. Yes!" she screamed, and the cry came from the deepest part of her being. "Fuck me!"

"All right, my dear. We have a slight change in plan, though. A much more enjoyable way of you reaching your little climax. You'll get all of the photographs, providing you follow directions."

It was the heat within her that made her answer through gritted teeth, "I'll do anything." She moaned helplessly as she moved her pelvis up and down, up and down, wanting to bring herself to final fruition.

Lord Drymuir twitched his cock again. In

response to her groan of delight, he said, "Yes... I guess you would do anything right now. I'm weary, my dear. I'll lie on the bottom, you shall be on top." Clasping her buttocks tightly in each hand, he rolled over, carrying Jenny with him. His cock stayed deeply buried in now wildly stretched vagina during the entire exercise.

Jenny propped her knees into the mattress, with his legs between her. Lord Drymuir used his hands to pull her buttocks down, then pushed her back up. "That's the way it's done," he said.

She rode his prick up and down and round and round as though she were aboard a carousel horse – her cunt reaching hopefully for the elusive brass ring of forbidden pleasure. She moaned in wild delight as she discovered that this new position permitted extra friction from his cock against her clitoris. It was beyond a doubt the most exciting thing she had ever felt in her life. She hated herself for what she was doing, yet knew it was impossible not to do it. She was his helpless slave now, even though she were on top and so free to dart away. The pictures were unimportant... the cock was the thing. She rode him unmercifully... bouncing up and down obscenely, flaunting her pelvis against the impaling shaft as though she were trying to drive it all the way through her body.

Through it all, Lord Drymuir lay there with an amused smile on his face; he even had his hands behind his head!

Jenny could feel everything coming together down there now. She was mixing ingredients that

– together – became a wild unstable compound which was threatening to explode at any moment. Her body was moving in abandoned wantonness. She was coming closer, closer, closer. She was moaning – mouthing incoherencies – and her eyes were rolling around in her head. Then Lord Drymuir's arms locked her in position! She was incapable of movement!

She stared down at him, wondering if he was ejaculating inside her, or if he had suddenly gone mad. Instead he was smiling mysteriously. Impatiently, she wiggled her ass a couple of time in an effort to get loose from his arms. He shook his head. "Relax, my dear. Here's where you get all of the pictures. Just lie still for a minute. Don't move."

Jenny felt obscene with her buttocks so nakedly exposed, but she did as instructed, feeling her inner muscles milking and massaging the warm cudgel inside her.

Suddenly, she felt a strange finger rubbing from her vagina to her anus!

She screamed and twisted around, then moaned in terror when she saw John McAlister beside the bed. He was completely naked; his thick cock was at full erection.

"Good evening, Jenny," John said formally, and pressured his wet finger into her tight puckered little anal ring.

"Oh, no... please no." Jenny panted. "You can't... it isn't right." She jerked and tried to rise.

"Hold her," John ordered, and Jenny felt Lord

Drymuir's arms lock again like a vise around her waist. Jenny screamed again, this time in pain, as the finger moved all the way in to its knuckle. She groaned as he began sawing it back and forth. Jenny attempted to get away from it by pressing down; this only skewered her cunt more deeply on Lord Drymuir's cock coming up from below.

She could feel the prick flexing inside of her. She tensed her buttocks tight in an effort to escape the finger; the action did nothing to halt McAlister's intrusion, but Lord Drymuir moaned in delight.

McAlister was kneading the left cheek of her ass with his hand. He kissed that sensitive spot below the base of her spine and bit her buttocks painfully. And all the time his finger sawed away monotonously in and out of her tightly clenched anal ring and into the warm, buttery depths of her rectum.

"Please... no," Jenny had begun, but then said, "Gaaaaggghh," as a second finger joined the first.

"Hurry, McAlister," Lord Drymuir commented. "She is nibbling me to sweet death. I do believe the young bitch has got me rather close to coming."

The pain in her anus and rectum was intense and burning. Jenny splayed her legs to avoid the pressure, but this only brought a third finger into play – all of them now making ever widening circles as her asshole was expanded ever wider.

Satisfied finally, McAlister climbed atop the bed. He peeled open her soft, yielding buttocks and then leaned forward to drop a larger drop of saliva which drooled down the smooth white crevice to her gaping anus.

He shuffled up between her and Lord Drymuir's legs. He clamped his hands on her hips. Then he pressed forward with his cock. Jenny fought it once again, but was held immovable by Lord Drymuir's arm and McAlister's grip. The head of McAlister's prick slipped easily into the already stretched anal opening; he kept right on going until his balls slapped up against her buttocks. "Unnnngggggghhhh!," she screamed, "you're killing me! Oh God, you're killing me!"

"Dear Jenny," McAlister said patiently, "you're being a child about this. You've enjoyed sodomy for the last two nights. This is merely a double exposure in return for the photographs."

"I say. A 'double exposure'. Rather good that," Lord Drymuir chuckled as he flexed his cock again. Jenny felt the responding twitch from McAlister.

McAlister began moving tentatively, "Gentle motions – those count in a young arsehole," he said philosophically.

Jenny felt as though someone had shoved pillows filled with rocks into her abdomen. Her bottom was filled, her cunt was filled. There was only a thin membrane separating the two phalluses, and they rubbed and bumped against each other like blindfolded wrestlers.

It was not long before the two men began buffeting her between them – as if she were a rag doll thrown in a game of "catch". She had never felt so helpless and naked before in her life. This was the end – whatever few grains of self-respect that may have been left in her mind were rapidly being consumed. Large wet tears streamed down both sides of her face to drop with a splash on Lord Drymuir's grey-haired chest. McAlister began driving in and out of her rectum with maniacal fury; Lord Drymuir was obviously close to coming... or dying of a heart attack! And Jenny? She could feel the pain being replaced by a kind of masochistic pleasure. Unable to escape... unable to prevent it... her body had no recourse but to accept.

And once again she lost control of her body! She could feel her orgasm coming back again... it seemed like the promise of bright sun behind moving clouds, flickers of warmth that came and went. Then, with frightening suddenness, it was there! It was she, who in her sudden desperate hunger, took control away from the two men; it was she who began frantically bucking against them, urging them on to harder and deeper thrusts. She reared her ass in the air to get full benefit of John McAlister's cock, then fell heavily skewering herself harder still down on George Drymuir's driving cock. "Fuck me," she screamed, "you fuckers... harder... harder... Oh God, fuck me harder!"

And it was her soprano scream that started the sweet upheaval first in her cunt, then seconds later in her rectum, and then in her clitoris. She came in all three places – achieved three different types of climaxes. And she continued to come for as long as the men would have her; until they fell from her in satiated weariness. Even above the glory of her orgasm, she felt a vague disappointment that the

double fucking of her well-stretched genitals had ended...

When it was over and the tears had dropped flowing, she lay nude for a long time just staring up at the ceiling. True - her body hurt, but the greatest pain was in her heart. They had stripped her of everything – pride, dignity, and faithfulness. They had made her a wanton adulteress, begging and screeching obscenities. They had used her body and – she knew this to be true – she had used them! They had made her reach climax after climax... something no one else had ever been able to do. She had given them something that her husband had never had.

And overall loomed the stunning, undeniable fact that she had enjoyed it... not the taunts, not the crawling or begging, or debasement and cruelty... but the sex act. That she had enjoyed... sex had been wonderful. Then she was weeping again as she realized what she must do to atone for the horrible sin of her wanton submission to two complete strangers.

CHAPTER ELEVEN

After an hour had passed and night had fallen, Bill knew he was hopelessly lost. His loud shouts of "hello" brought no response. He knew he would be safe if he could find the road, so he began walking in a direction that he thought would lead out of the woods. Twice, in the stillness of the night, the sound of dogs came. Once, he stumbled upon a herd of wild boar and was forced to climb a tree to get away from an enraged tusker. The animal snorted and clawed the ground, and stared up with baleful red eyes. Twice, its yellow tusks gleaming in the moonlight, the animal charged the tree. A persistent bastard, it remained there for almost an hour.

When it finally ambled off, so did Bill!

It was almost eleven before he found the road and began walking. He had walked almost three miles before a black figure came hurtling out of the night at him. He leaped aside and shouted, "You idiot. You almost ran over me." The figure on a bicycle turned around to stare, then wobbled crazily, and crashed into the ditch.

"Now, you see what you've done," a Scottish voice complained. "Ye've wrecked ma new bike. And ma wife will think I did it because o' the drink."

Bill, feeling foolish because he had been half-frightened out of his wits, was immediately contrite. "Look, I'm sorry. I'm lost. You scared hell out of me – coming over the top of the hill that way, without lights. I thought Old Nick had finally caught up with me."

The local rubbed the seat of his pants where he had landed after the crash. He looked at Bill. "Ay, ye've a right tae be wurried about the Divil on this road. He's been seen monny a time by those who were sober." He shuddered, and then bent down to pick up his bike. "Och, it looks in fair shape.

Mebbe nae harm's been done at that. Where are ye bound this time o' night?"

"I'm lost. I went hunting... got separated from my party. I'm staying at Castle Strathblane."

The man tensed. "Well then, I'll expect ye'll have nae need to fear the Divil. Good night, sir."

Bill was puzzled by the man's attitude, but he let it pass. "Can you tell me how to get back?"

His new friend jerked his head in the direction Bill was headed. "Three miles up the road and turn tae the right." He hesitated, then said in a more friendly manner, "And guid luck tae ye. A friend o' the owner's?"

"No... merely a guest. Why?"

The man took a deep breath and drew himself up; when he exhaled, it was obvious that he had been drinking. "You look a bright lad. Are ye honeymooning?"

"Yes."

"Then tak ma advice and leave. Strange things happen in yon wicked place. People complain o' strange dreams in which the Divil takes part. Only this Spring a new bride o' just four days lept to her death from the towers. And none of the local girls will work there. And more than one young couple has arrived together and departed separately... or much earlier than planned." He threw a leg over the bike's seat. "One thing I know, I'd never leave ma own bride there... alone." He rode quickly off into the darkness.

Bill stared after him. What a lot of nonsense, he thought. "Strange things", "suicides", and "strange dreams", typical superstitious clap-trap, from an Scot who has had too much to drink.

He had taken half a dozen paces before he stopped and said aloud, "Strange dreams?" He abruptly recalled the dreams about Mary before he finally found himself in the sack with her. Come to think of it, Jenny had been acting oddly all day... almost as if she had been worried about something. He quickened his pace and, by the time he reached the turn-off, he was actually jogging.

It was midnight when he arrived; the castle was completely dark except for lights shining from the windows of their suite. "Thank God," he breathed, "Jenny's up... and okay."

Rather than awaken the house by going to the front door and ringing the bell, he decided to go around to the servants entrance and enter through the storage area. Once inside, the darkness was oppressive. He fumbled his way through the room, and was relieved to find a door which lead to the dimly lighted hallway. Quickly he made his way up the servants back stairs. When he reached the third floor, he turned toward what he thought was his suite. He was halfway down the corridor, in front of a statue of a knight in armour, when he suddenly discovered he was in the wrong wing. There, in front of him, was the room he had come from last night... when he had mysteriously awakened next to Mary. He spun around, and as he did so, his jacket sleeve caught on the handle of the knight's sword. There was a whispering noise and a door silently opened in the blank wall.

Bill stepped back in surprise and momentary fright, tensed and waiting for someone to come through. When no one appeared, his eyes narrowed and he reached out to push the sword and scabbard. The door closed. He pushed up on the sword; the door swung open again.

Peering around to make sure no one was watching, Bill quickly stepped through the opening. It whispered shut behind him. He spun rapidly, feeling trapped, but as the door closed, the lights came on automatically. Alongside the door was a lever. He touched it; the lights went out, the door opened. He closed the door again and, as the lights came up, he began an inspection.

At one turning, he saw what appeared to be a pane of clear glass. Someone was moving behind the glass. When he got closer, he realized it must be some sort of trick mirror, for it was obvious that the weeping and wildly gesticulating nude Lady Liza had no idea that he was there. The nude Scottish maid was screeching at Lady Liza. Suddenly, her temper boiling, the girl picked up a broad leather belt and began beating the older woman who rolled and pleaded on the floor. "A couple of lesbians fighting, serves the old bitch right," was his disinterested comment. He walked on until he came to what seemed to be almost a theatre lounge with several leather chairs placed strategically in front of another window. There was a tripod standing there also. When Bill looked down through the glass, he almost passed out from the sudden shock. He could see Mary, her hair in curlers, reading a book in bed. Even as he watched, she yawned, closed the book, took a drink of water from the night glass, and turned off the light.

Oh, my God! he thought in sudden dismay. Was anyone up here last night when she and I...?

Suspicion was piling up on suspicion. It was with a pounding heart and oppressive feeling of apprehension that Bill began moving back toward the secret passage. He made a wrong turn once, opened a door, and found himself in a well-equipped modern darkroom. Several rolls of film hung from a drying line. Quickly he exited, and a moment later was outside in the wing hallway again. He closed the door, then stood there for a moment trying to catch his thoughts. What kind of crazy operation was this anyway? Lesbians. Trick mirrors? Were McAlister, Mary and Drymuir some kind of perverts who got their kicks out of watching other people make love? He thought about what Mary had said concerning his demand for oral sex. Had anyone seen that? "Oh, my God," he repeated, this time with more than desperation in his voice.

"We've got to get out of this loonybin tonight," he said aloud, making an immediate decision. He didn't know what he'd tell Jenny, but if necessary he would force her to pack at once.

All the lights were on in their suite when he entered. Jenny, looking pale and distraught, was dressed in her travelling clothes. Her bags were packed. She turned to him and her composure disintegrated; she began weeping as soon as she saw him.

"Jenny? What's wrong?" he asked, suddenly very frightened and positive that someone had told her about Mary. He started toward her.

"Bill, don't touch me. Don't come near me. I'm leaving you. I would have gone earlier, but there was no way of getting to the railway unless you drove me."

"Jenny..." it was a plea, wrenched out of him. "What are you talking about?"

"I can't stay with you."

Bill swallowed. So... she did know about his adulterous behaviour with Mary. He could barely speak because of the sudden tightness in his throat. "It was something I did?" the question croaked out of him.

Huge tears boiled up in her eyes; she refused to look at him. Finally she took a deep shuddering breath and answered, "No, my darling. Nothing you've done."

"Then what?"

She shook her head. Bill, suddenly angry at the uncertainty of the whole situation, darted across the room and roughly grabbed her shoulders. "You just can't leave like that. I'm your husband. You're my wife. I demand to know what's wrong!" The last was shouted.

Jenny closed her eyes, the tears continued to stream down her face. Her shoulders slumped. "All right. You're entitled to know exactly what kind of a person you married. You made a mistake! Go home. Get an annulment. You thought I was decent. I'll show you. I'll show you what you married. It is going to hurt you. If you kill me I won't complain. I deserve it. Your hurt from seeing this will go away in time, but I'll have to live with it festering inside me for the rest of my life."

"What in hell are you talking about?"

Shuddering, Jenny reached into her purse and pulled out the manila envelope. She gave it to him.

Bill unfastened the clasp and withdrew the photographs. His eyes widened in horror and disgust as he looked at the first one. He looked sick by the time he had rifled through the stack. His mind was whirling; he didn't believe it. This was all a mad dream... a dream? And knowing beyond a doubt that someone somewhere in the castle had photographs of him too, he mumbled, "Oh... God!"

Jenny collapsed, weeping. Between sobs she managed to say, "You see... why I can't stay married to you?"

There were things to be done. The first thing he wanted to do was kill George Drymuir and John McAlister. The second? The second... No, there was something far more important than revenge. Jenny!

He put his hand gently under the chin and lifted her sweet face. She tried to turn away from him, but he wouldn't let her go. "Darling. Listen to me," he pleaded. "Did you know you were doing this? I mean... did you dream you were doing it?"

Sobbing, she merely nodded. "In my dream I was doing it with you... and it was so... beautiful and right."

"You couldn't help doing this. You were drugged... or, more likely, under hypnotic suggestion or something."

"Bill, those pictures were taken last night. Tonight, though, I wasn't hypnotized. I did everyone of those things all over again tonight. They made me. They said they would give me the photographs if I did it. They said I had to do it or they would show you the pictures. They were going to send copies to my mother, to everyone in my address book..."

"Blackmail."

"Yes," her body shuddered. "But they made me... they did things to me that made me... lose control of myself." She looked up, her eyes filled with shame. "You should know the truth. They made me beg... and I begged. Don't you understand? They called me a slut and a whore... and I am... because they did things to me that made me want to... I wanted to... to..." She closed her eyes, and all the life drained out of her. "When they gave me the photographs, it was only then that they told me I would have to do 'other' things for the negatives."

The word "negative" did it for Bill. He suddenly realized what his mind – his memory! – had been trying to tell him for minutes. The dark room! Of course! The negative would be there. And, if there were negatives of Jenny, there would be others of other people. Enough negatives to let the police know what was going on. There might even be negatives of the girl who committed suicide. And, abruptly, Bill knew he didn't really want to kill McAlister and Drymuir; that was too easy – and much too good for them. They enjoyed their little games with innocent people. Cage them both up in prison – without sex – for long years and it would be, literally, a fate worse than death.

Bill turned to his sobbing wife. "Jenny," he snapped, "now listen to me. No more talk about annulment or leaving me. We... you and I... are getting out of here right now. And we're taking the negatives with us. If you still want a divorce or annulment after we get away from this place, I won't stop you. But we are leaving together. Right now. Understand? Pack my bags. Do it quickly. Take them downstairs and out the back way to the garage. Be very quiet. Will you do as I say?"

For the first time since he had entered there was a shadow of hope in her eyes. "But how could you stand to live with me, knowing what I am?"

"We'll talk about that later. Just do as I say."

Wide-eyed, Jenny nodded, slowly at first and then with increasing hope. When Bill left the room a minute later, she was already opening his dresser drawer.

He went surely through the walls, hesitating only when he reached the McAlister's wing. No one stirred. He moved the sword and the door opened. A second later, he passed the window overlooking Lady Liza's room. The maid had tied Lady Liza to the bedpost. A long black whip lay on the bedspread and the Scottish maid, screaming obscenities at the tearfully pleading butch dyke, was viciously sodomizing her with the ten-inch dildo. The girl apparently had squeezed the hot-water balls because a thin stream of defecation and water ran down the inner thighs of both of them.

Bill didn't pause to watch the lewd spectacle; truly, he thought, this was the "Divil's castle" just as the local drunk had said.

Once in the darkroom, he gave silent thanks for McAlister's scientific method of operation. Every print was numbered in a negative book, so it took only a minute to discover that six prints had been made of Jenny. Those would be the six prints given to her.

There had been, much to his chagrin, five prints made of him. Where were they? That was the question. Who had them? Then he caught sight of the small notation, "To N." So Mary had them? The negative book also showed that there had been a total of seven rolls of film shot of Jenny and him. He looked up on the drying line; there were seven stripes of film hanging there. He scanned them in the light; yes, they were the right ones. Two of the rolls were of Mary down on him in fellatio, of him performing cunnilingus on her, of the two of them indulging in soixante-neuf, and of wild frenzied fucking between the two of them. He shoved the negatives in his pockets, then buttoned the pockets to make sure the film did not fall out.

The negative book was a very interesting document. There were names and dates and – in a few places – even sums of money listed. Bill decided it would make excellent evidence for the police... that, together with the other negatives. There were two filing cases loaded with them. Many of the pictures obviously went back to the time when McAlister had operated in London as a gynecologist. No wonder he had been able to buy the castle!

It took Bill four trips to carry all of the negatives to the car. When he completed the fourth trip, Jenny was sitting in the front seat waiting for him. "What are all those boxes," she asked.

"Photographic negatives, darling, of poor ignorant unsuspecting people like you and me." When he said "me", Bill realized he had almost forgotten the photographs delivered to Mary.

"Be very quiet," he said. "I'll be back in ten minutes or so." He had made his way halfway across the courtyard when the dogs came at him barking. A moment later, the lights came on in the courtyard, and McAlister opened his window on the third floor to shout down, "Who's there?"

Bill was caught. There was no way he could escape notice. He stepped boldly out into the light and looked up. "Hi, John. It's me. I got lost... had a helluva time finding my way back."

McAlister shouted, "Thank God, you're safe. We'll call off the search. We've been looking everywhere for you. We were frantic with worry."

"You lying son of a bitch," Bill said under his breath, then shouted up, "Don't bother to come down. I'll let myself in... and go right to bed. Boy, am I ever tired."

"Good show. See you tomorrow."

"Make it late, will you. Don't have anyone wake us up early. I want to sleep in. I've walked five hundred miles tonight, it seems."

"Right-o." The courtyard went out. Bill looked back toward the car; Jenny's face was only a white blur in the dimness. He held up his finger to his mouth in a charade of silence.

The racket probably had awakened Mary, he thought; if so, we'll just have to bluff it. When he reached the third floor landing, he listened carefully and then slowly tip-toed toward Mary's room. Quietly he pushed the door open; the room was dark, and it smelled of Mary's perfume. He could hear her rhythmic breathing; she was asleep.

It took him almost ten agonizing minutes before he found the packet of photographs in a drawer beneath her undergarments. Quickly he counted the pictures; they were all there. With the treasure safely inside his coat pocket, he relaxed enough to lose some of his caution. That was when he knocked over the table lamp.

"Who's there?" Mary sat bolt upright in bed.

"Shhhh," Bill whispered. "It's me."

"Bill?" she hissed. "What are you doing here?"

"Why do you think? I can't go to sleep without you. I keep remembering how you felt... how you taste."

He heard her breath expel in animal eagerness. "Have you been to your room yet?" she asked, almost breathlessly.

"Yes. Jenny's asleep. She won't miss me. She won't miss this long hard thing I've got for you."

Mary groaned deep in her throat; obviously her body was rapidly coming to life. "You're sure you want me?" she asked.

"I want you so badly that I'm going to get down on my hands and knees in front of you and I'm going to... going to..."

"Yes... Yes! Don't talk about it. Do it. Do it. Do it!" He could hear her panting; the heat had come on her that quickly. She threw the blanket and sheet from her and began struggling out of her gown.

Bill tried to sound equally excited; he made short gasps of what he hoped would pass as impatience. Then he said, "Oh, damn!"

"What is it? What is it?"

"Mary, I have to go back to the room for a second. I felt the water running. I'll be right back."

"God-damnit, hurry then!" In the dim glow of her illuminated clock he could see her fumbling with her curlers.

"I will... meanwhile you just think about what it's going to feel like when I start biting, when I slip this thing into you." He saw her legs clench together in passionate impatience, and then he quickly left the room.

He reached the top of the stairs and turned back to look in the direction of Mary's bedroom. He grinned. He tossed her a kiss. "Just keep thinking about it, baby. Think about it... all night... long."

The dogs met him at the front door, but they remained silent this time, wagging their tails and frolicking alongside him. They continued to play with him while he pushed the car down the road, and through the front gates, and across the little stone bridge. Then they were rolling free down a small incline. When he reached the turn in the road hiding them from the castle, Bill put the car in gear and started the engine.

They drove up... up... up the hill, then swung around a curve. For a moment, the moon glittered and skipped on the loch, while the castle looked as though it were made of moonlit gossamer, a ghostly apparition from the past rather than the solid stone edifice that it really was... then it disappeared from sight.

Jenny fought it, but began weeping again.

Bill patted her knee. He had never felt so confident in his life. What he planned to do might be a horrible mistake; but he knew it was their only chance. He reached into his inside pocket and pulled out a manila envelope. "Here. These probably won't make you feel any better, but they may change your mind about a lot of things."

He heard her gasp as she saw the first picture, then additional intakes of breath as she came across each new scene. She turned to him, her eyes full of questions... and uncertainty. "Bill? You look as if... like you were..."

"Enjoying it?"

"Yes."

"I was."

"But how could you?"

"Simple. I thought I was giving pleasure to you... just as you thought you were pleasuring me."

Jenny was silent as she put the pictures back in the envelope. She remained silent, pensive, as they drove into the night. She said nothing when, three hours later, they arrived in Glasgow. Bill stopped in front of the central police station went to speak to the duty officer. "I think you'll find the reason for a girl's suicide at Castle Strathblane six months ago... plus I'm sure the London police and Scotland Yard will be very interested in the older photographs together with the sums of money indicated." Having assured the man he would be willing to act as a witness, he returned to the car.

She sat there dazed, as Bill engaged the clutch and drove off towards the airport. In the East, the sky was lightening and a new day approached.

On the journey they had stopped to burn their photographs and the rolls of film shot of them. The ashes were thrown into the cleansing waters of a loch and disappeared from sight.

At the airport they booked in to an ordinary hotel. Too tired to do more than collapse into bed together, they slept like logs until late in the following morning.

"'Morning, sleepy-head!"
Jenny looked up into the clear, sparkling eyes of her handsome husband. Was it really him? She pinched herself. Yes, she was definitely awake. This was no hypnotic half-dream. He kissed her lovingly on her forehead, on her nose, and then on her lips. She responded by drawing him to her, feeling his

strong, masculine frame as it reassuringly covered her own, softer, more feminine body. Her mouth opened to his and their tongues danced: advancing and retreating, they played together in the most deliciously intimate and sensual way. Jenny felt the first warming flickers of arousal as her loins suddenly came alive. Little sparks of desire raced to and from her erogenous zones, connecting them in tiny rivulets of flowing, liquid fire.

Bill slipped his hand knowingly between her thighs. She was wet. Very wet. Then Jenny reciprocated tentatively, her small hand encircling his sleeping giant of a cock, already more than half-hard, but not completely stiff. It surged and pulsed in her fingers, increasing her desire. *I need to be fucked by my husband,* she thought. *I need to have real sex with my real husband, not some phantasmagorical, hallucinatory, fraudulent illusion of him.*

I want to feel his cock in my pussy... no my wet, needful... cunt. Somehow this blunt, dirty word seemed to match her lascivious mood. *I need to be filled where there is now just an aching void, and when I've come I want him to...*

Jenny's thoughts tailed off... what exactly *did* she want? Blushing, she remembered just how much she loved to have her buttocks parted, her anus penetrated and then her rectum filled with a solid length of hard, male meat, how it was enough to make her come. And her handsome husband had never taken her there. Surely, it was time to change that.

"I want you to fuck me, Bill," she whispered in her husband's ear. "Then I want you to bugger me. Bugger me until I come."

Bill looked at his wife, astounded. His hand worked her wet pussy, his fingers slipping between the slippery folds, playing with the hard bud of her clitoris. At this lascivious, inflammatory invitation, his great cock surged to rock-hardness in a second.

Jenny opened her thighs wide in unmistakable erotic welcome. She guided his cock until it docked at the mouth of her clamouring, needy cunt. Then she dug her fingers into his tight, muscular buns and pulled him towards her. It took all of five powerful thrusts for her to reach her first orgasm. She expressed herself loudly, joyfully. And Bill kept thrusting until she had three further climaxes and she begged him to stop... but not for too long.

"More? But, honey, at this rate you'll wake the whole hotel!"

Jenny just laughed a low, sexy laugh and struggled to her knees.

"Well, we better do something else, then."

She stuck her shapely bottom into the air. Reaching back with her hands, she pulled her luscious nether cheeks apart and flexed her anus teasingly at him. Bill's eyes were on stalks. His beautiful blonde wife was inviting him to assfuck her. Just above her dripping, lust-inflamed cuntlips, he could see her neat little brown asshole winking lewdly.

"Like what you see?" she simpered.

"Oh yes, honey," he replied, fervently, "it's

every man's dream of pure heaven..."

Kneeling close behind her, Bill sluiced his outsized stiff cock up and down her vaginal slit a couple of times to lubricate it as much as possible, then started to slowly ease the head into her twitching little anal ring.

As the head of her husband's cock finally slid past the tight ring of her anal sphincter, Jenny gave a groan of deep fulfilment. And then she did something that surprised even her. She thrust her luscious buttocks back towards him, violently impaling herself upon his enormous cock until she could feel the heavy balls in his wrinkled scrotal sac slap against her wet pussylips.

Her eyes bulged, her mouth flew open and her face contorted with a fleeting pain, but the sensations of acute discomfort soon transmuted into ones of sensory bliss: any twinges of pain were soon subsumed by heavenly feelings provided by her husband's thrusting cock.

So slowly, gently, Bill began to bugger his bride; the brown outer pigmentation of her anus disappeared with every thrust in, and the bubblegum-pink flesh of her anal interior clasped and clung to his huge member every time he withdrew.

The tempo increased, and soon the newlyweds were groaning and crying in pure ecstatic lust as they coupled energetically together until Bill could take it no more. His features were set in a grimacing mask – eloquent proof of the agonizingly intense sensations of his impending orgasm. He pulled out as if to spurt his cumload over Jenny's back.

But to his amazement, his young wife wheeled around and seized his quivering prick in both hands and brought it to her face, jerking it with an expertise born more of intuition than experience until jets of thick white sperm spurted from the tip of his cock. Then, to Bill's increasing surprise, the young blonde quickly slipped her lips over the jerking, spurting glans of his cock, seemingly oblivious of its last port of call, and sucked him gently as he finished ejaculating inside the warm wet cave of her mouth. She was forced to swallow several times before he finally completed his orgasm.

Bill collapsed back on to the bed and lay there, blissfully, utterly, satiated, as his lovely young wife snuggled up to him, a small hand still cupping his softening phallus and his scrotum in a sweet, proprietorial way. Somehow the relief they both felt at their new-found sexual compatability was compensation enough for the ordeal of the last few days. As the sunlight streamed though the curtains, it felt to both of them not so much like the beginning of just a new day in each other's company, but the start of a whole, wonderful new life together.

THE END

Become an *Eroti*

Review Subscriber

Payment is simple – by credit card or cheque
Internet:
www.eroticreviewmagazine.com
Our friendly, free orderline:
0800 026 25 24
Subscribe by email:
leadline@eroticprints.org

THE OBSESSION ISSUE
WHEN DOES SEX BECOME TOO MUCH OF A GOOD THING?
OFF WITH THE CHOPPER JAPANESE STYLE
ON THE SET: PLAYBOY PORNO SHOOT
FELICIEN ROPS AT SOTHEBY'S
BAYLEY ON CARS AS SEX OBJECTS

JESSICA RODER

THROUGH A GLASS DARKLY...
A PHOTOGRAPHIC JOURNEY
OF SEXUAL DISCOVERY

The Young Governess in Egypt

The sequel to the best-selling *The Young Governess*, by Phoebe Gardener. Upon the death of her lover, the eponymous heroine decides to visit Egypt, accompanied by her bi-sexual companion, Ruth. There a whole series of wild sexual adventures await them, including an erotic journey up th Nile, capture by Bedouin slave traders, and a magical stay in a rich man's harem.

Shameful Duties

Mary and Jessica Douglas, an attractive Chinese mother-and-daughter team desperately seek financial security. And they're prepared to get it, at almost any price. So when Victor Jordan, Fairview's richest man, courts Jessie, Mom is thrilled. However, the worst sort of sexual degradation awaits them both.

Havana Harlot

The daughter of millionaire businessman, Charlie, gets kidnapped on a family holiday in Cuba. In an attempt to defy the kidnappers, Charlie unintentionally causes his whole family to become the sexual playthings of the gang and they are forced to perform acts of unspeakable depravity with one another.

To order these PAST VENUS PRESS and any other titles:

Orderline: 0800 026 25 24
Email: leadline@eroticprints.org
Post: EPS, 54 New Street,
Worcester WR1 2DL

ERB

WWW.EROTICPRINTS.ORG

THE BANKER'S WIFE

John Barbour

Funny how an innocent encounter can turn people's lives upside-down. When Harry and Diane Laurence 'clicked' with Max and Penny Byron at the year's dullest cocktail party, it might have gone no further than improving a potentially ghastly evening for these attractive couples. But the sexually sophisticated Byrons like to swing, and once they'd targeted the innocent young Laurences, the banker and his wife won't rest until they've scored – big time. Moreover, the banker's bisexual wife wants to play with both husband *and* wife. Penny is a beautiful, dangerous woman, just as predatory as her affluent, randy husband, while Diane Laurence's almost virginal naiveté and her husband's lack of experience leaves her totally exposed to this older couple's fiendish machinations.

Orderline: 0800 026 25 24
Email: leadline@eroticprints.org
Post: EPS, 54 New Street, Worcester WR1 2DL

ERB

WWW.EROTICPRINTS.ORG

THE RAVISHED AMERICAN BRIDE

Bob Stainer

When Edward Tremayne brings Molly, his pretty new American bride, back to Cornwall, he warns her that his folks are not quite like others. Indeed, she is not expecting Firethorn, a large, imposing period house crammed to the eves with her delightful adult in-laws. Young Molly soon falls victim to the charm of her handsome father-in-law Piers, and his wife, Georgina, who looks almost the same age as their teenage children. But on the very first night of her stay she discovers a family secret that pulls her down into a spiral of decadent lust and depravity...

With oral, anal, and lesbian action, group incest, orgies and non-stop sex, this is a superb erotic tale in the setting of the lush English countryside. With superb illustrations by Tom Sargent.

Orderline: 0800 026 25 24
Email: leadline@eroticprints.org
Post: EPS, 54 New Street, Worcester WR1 2DL

WWW.EROTICPRINTS.ORG

ACADEMY
OF
LUST
Jenny Strong

Emily and Olivia Newbridge are heirs to a fabulously wealthy business empire that, one day, 22-year-old Emily is determined to run. Both sisters lack social skills, so their guardians send 18-year-old Olivia to a Swiss finishing school while Emily's employers invite her to a weekend seminar. Shockingly, both sisters are subjected to every sadistic torment and humiliation in the book! In their separate punishment worlds, they are forced to experience corporal punishment, public defloration, and many appalling perversions. But their bondage hells become submissive heavens and they gradually learn how to enjoy sex – on their own terms...

Featuring corporal punishment, bondage, defloration, urination and non-consensual sex, *Academy of Lust* suits a sophisticated erotic taste and is a superb BDSM read.